"Not so fast," she said, and moved her lips to Cody's, kissing her lightly, teasingly.

Cody drew a ragged breath, caught hold of Annabel's hips and pulled her determinedly toward the bed.

"Why not fast?" she said, throwing back the covers and drawing Annabel down with her. She felt sick with passion, wanted Annabel inside her, around her, close and hot.

Annabel's hands were on her shoulders, pressing them down, as she knelt across Cody's body, astride one thigh so Cody could feel her wetness. She bent to kiss Cody's face, just brushing the skin with her lips until Cody's mouth parted, trembling and full, and she whispered Annabel's name, then gasped as fingers found her clitoris, slid down to sample her wetness then moved casually back again.

Cody lifted her hips, wanting more than the slow teasing strokes. She opened heavy eyes and met Annabel's, dark, intense purple, the pupils dilated. She reached up, slid her fingers into Annabel's hair and pulled her down to kiss her passionately, reveling in the foreign textures of her body. Her breasts felt firm, the nipples hard. She was hot and smooth, as supple as a cat.

Passion Bay

by Jennifer Fulton

Passion Bay

by Jennifer Fulton

The Naiad Press, Inc.
1994

Printed in the United States of America on acid-free paper
First Edition
First Printing June 1992
Second Printing July 1993
Third Printing October 1994

Edited by Claire McNab and Katherine V. Forrest
Cover design by Pat Tong and Bonnie Liss
   (Phoenix Graphics)
Typeset by Sandi Stancil

Library of Congress Cataloging-in-Publication Data

Fulton, Jennifer, 1958–
  Passion bay / by Jennifer Fulton.
     p.   cm.
  ISBN 1-56280-028-0
  I. Title.
PS3566.U524P37   1992
813′.54—dc20

91-38096
CIP

About the Author

Jennifer Fulton is a full-time writer. She lives in Wellington, New Zealand with her partner, daughter and numerous animal companions. When she's not writing, you can find her up the nearest river with her fly rod, catching trout.

For my beloved H.

CHAPTER ONE

Mid-winter bus-stop conversation was cheerless and predictable, half-sentences captured before the wind could steal them away, people's faces mottled, noses dripping. Like a family of fat grey caterpillars, the commuters inched their way along Lambton Quay platform, clutching the jetsam of their working lives in briefcases and plastic shopping bags, and glaring at the derelict spread full-length along one of the few benches available.

The bus was late, of course. It would have caused needless shock and distress if it arrived on time.

There would have been nothing to talk about except the weather, and it did seem pointless to tell someone engaged in a death struggle with coat and scarf that it was a lousy day.

Wellington, New Zealand, was a vile city in July. Southerly winds roared straight up from the Antarctic, constant earth tremors made the entire office population nervous and twitchy, and the suicide rate doubled.

Cody Stanton hated it. She hated the endless greyness of it all, the flu that everyone had in one form or another, the traffic accidents and the sirens screaming all day. She hated the litter blowing unnoticed along the street, the deadened faces of pedestrians, the television screens in shop windows playing nothing but rugby.

Someone gave her a shove and she realized the queue in front of her had vanished. Hurrying forward, she ran agitated fingers through her wind-battered hair and hoisted herself up the unfriendly steps onto the trolleybus.

"Two sections," she muttered, and for once failed to notice the driver's thighs or her assessing look.

The bus lurched away while she was stumbling down the aisle and Cody caught her leather jacket on an old woman's shopping trundler and trod right across the protruding Reeboked feet of a brawny youth. She heard his *Fuck you then* without registering it, and headed for the only empty seat in the bus, right at the back beside a large Indian woman. Careful not to wreck the filmy sari spilling from the woman's raincoat, she occupied the child-sized space next to her and stared sightlessly ahead.

People got made redundant every day, of course. Only somehow Cody had thought it would never happen to her. She had a nice safe job in computers and her particular skills were in short supply in the technology-shy New Zealand market. Redundancy wasn't going to look too hot on her CV, she realized. There were people at work who had actually resigned to avoid that stigma; men, of course, shit scared of taking a nosedive in the job market. Fortunately she wasn't too proud to take a redundancy check, Cody thought, feeling for the reassuring stiffness of the envelope in her pocket.

She hadn't opened it yet. Packing up her desk had been traumatic enough in the half hour they'd all been given. Clear out your belongings and leave the building. Cody couldn't believe it. Treated like criminals, somebody said. They weren't supposed to speak to the other staff or notice the awkward looks; sympathy coupled with fear. Cody could remember feeling that same queasy relief herself, when the first redundancies were announced several months back. She had watched colleagues depart, some of them with few prospects in their own specialties. Many had moved overseas, one had killed himself. Losing his job was not the main reason, the staff psychologist had insisted. There were personal problems . . .

Cody squeezed her way off the bus at the Hataitai shops and, despite the wind and rain, took the longest route to her flat. Once there, she

3

lingered at the gate on another silly pretext. Last night it had been paint flakes on the footpath, tonight her shoelaces needed tightening. *Fool,* she thought, and forced herself determinedly along the path and up to her front door. She pushed it open with a pounding heart, half expecting to smell food cooking and hear some scratchy old Ferron recording. But the narrow passageway was dark and silent, the air stale with last night's fish and chips.

For the first time that day, tears crept down Cody's cheeks. She brushed them away impatiently. If Margaret had been there she would have rushed down to the kitchen, burst out with her news, thrust the check at her lover to open and leaned up against her, warm and safe. But instead she wandered into the emptiness of her room, dropped her satchel and curled up on her bed staring at the discolored patch of wall where Margaret's Amelia Earhart poster had hung.

She really ought to hang something else there, Cody thought for about the twentieth time in two weeks. But instead she lay motionless and icy cold until darkness swallowed the outline on the wallpaper and made a black hole of the gap where Margaret's chest of drawers had once squatted, drawers neatly packed, doilies arranged on top.

She should make some dinner, Cody realized, only there was nothing in the house. She hadn't bothered to shop since Margaret left. Anyway, she didn't have much of an appetite today, especially not for greasies again.

With a listless shrug she flicked on the lamp, pulled the envelope from her pocket and tore off one end. A message on heavy embossed letterhead informed her that she had redundancy compensation of $10,000 and a check was stapled to the back. Cody pried it off and looked at it. Then her brow creased and she rubbed her eyes. She counted the zeros and read it out loud. *"One hundred thousand dollars."*

For a moment she panicked, then looked at it again. "Shit!" she whispered. "A hundred grand." Still the same. Those stupid bastards in Admin had messed up. Now she'd have to gird her loins and march straight back in there tomorrow to sort it all out.

"This is not my day," she said as she crawled under the quilt with her clothes on.

When the sun hit Cody's face the next morning, she opened her eyes with a shock and threw off her bedclothes. Eight-thirty! She was late. Cursing, she hurtled toward the bathroom, then remembered. On the floor beside her bed lay an oblong slip of paper. Cody approached it as though it were radioactive and stared down at the neatly typed figures. Even upside down, even in the clear light of day, they were still the same. *One hundred thousand dollars.*

Of course she'd have to give it back. Admin had probably discovered their mistake already and canceled it. But what if they hadn't? What if they'd just stamped her file *processed* and shoved it back to Records in this week's big stack of redundancies?

Cody scooped the check up from the floor and brushed imaginary dust off it. What if she kept it, spent it? That would serve the bastards right, she thought a little wildly. What could they do? Ask her for $90,000 back please? Put her in jail?

For the first time in two weeks, Cody laughed.

Later that morning, the bank teller was less amused.

"Large deposit," he commented, looking Cody over as if she were in a police line-up.

"Been made redundant," she said, suitably tragic.

His face cleared immediately and he rearranged his expression into one of pious concern. "Very sorry," he murmured with a shake of the head. "Lot of it about."

Cody did her best to look nonchalant as he keyed in the deposit and rubber-stamped everything. She could almost feel the security cameras zooming in on her, see her face immortalized on TV screens all over New Zealand in *Crimewatch* — Cody Stanton, female Caucasian aged 28, 5'7", slim build, black hair and grey eyes. Wanted for theft. She shivered.

The teller was speaking to her in a confiding tone. "... lot of money. Our manager can advise ... don't hesitate to call ..."

"Thank you." Cody shoveled her deposit book into her bag. "I certainly shall. You've been most helpful." Bestowing her best school-photo smile on him, she escaped.

"A hundred grand," she muttered under her breath as she walked away from the bank. Now what?

🙠 🙠 🙠 🙠 🙠

6

Seven thousand miles away Annabel Worth was burying her aunt. It was a small private ceremony and she was one of a handful of mourners who tossed carnations onto the coffin as it was lowered. Glancing about, she recognized a couple of distant cousins and several tearful older women, friends of her aunt's. Annabel's parents were represented by a lavish wreath in the shape of a cross. The closest they could come to having the last word, she guessed cynically. Her aunt would have hated it, pagan that she was.

When the priest had finished, Annabel slowly approached the edge of the grave, her black Bally heels sinking into the soft lawn. People were drifting away in twos and threes, probably returning to their hotels to prepare for the discreet gathering later in the day. The sun seemed indecently bright. Annie would never see it again, her niece thought sadly. She took a handful of earth and released it onto the gleaming coffin. A dead woman in a dead tree ... This time she pushed a clod down with her foot. It made a soft, distinctive thud and Annabel stared after it, wanting to cry, but tearless.

"Miss Worth?" The voice behind her made her turn quickly. She was faced by a short, perspiring young man who thrust a damp card at her.

"Jessup. Bryan Jessup of Swain, Buddle, Jessup," he told her. "Walter Jessup's my father," he added, as though that explained everything.

"You are a lawyer, I take it," Annabel said dryly and retreated from the grave's edge.

"We are," her companion confirmed loftily.

Annabel waited. He just stood there staring as though confronted with a rare zoo specimen.

7

"What may I do for you, Mr. Jessup?" she finally prompted.

"Oh ... yes ... I'm sorry." He cleared his throat. "I wonder whether we might arrange an appointment to discuss your late aunt's affairs."

Annabel raised an eyebrow. Her aunt's affairs. Now that would make for interesting conversation. But not with a sweaty young California lawyer, she decided. What on earth did Swain and so forth want with her anyway?

"I'm afraid I don't quite understand, Mr. Jessup," she said in dignified old Boston. It produced immediate results.

"Of course." He mopped his forehead. "I do apologize, Miss Worth. Your aunt's untimely death must have come as a great shock to you." He glanced over her shoulder with obvious discomfort. "Perhaps I could er ... walk you to your car ... drive you to your hotel."

"Thank you." Annabel regretted it immediately. The last thing she felt like was trying to keep her close fitting black silk skirt over her knees while Jessup, Junior drove all over San Francisco.

She reluctantly followed him to a white Porsche; doubtless his father's, she though unkindly. He opened the door with a flourish and attempted to assist her in, but Annabel shook him off. Typical, she thought, settling into her seat. She'd never met a man yet who didn't behave like a fool around her, staring as if he'd never seen a blonde in a country that had cornered the world peroxide market.

Ever since childhood people had stared at her, some even assuming they had some automatic right to touch her. For years she had loathed her appearance, her unhealthy pale skin, her peculiar pinky-blue eyes and the hair that was blonder than Barbie's. Other girls paraded about in bikinis — and she wore a sundress. With sleeves. Other girls could wear makeup. On Annabel it looked as stark as paint.

Her painful self-consciousness had never quite vanished, even after she'd "successfully" married. What a dismal mistake that had been. How naive she'd been back then, Annabel thought cynically.

After avoiding males throughout high school and college, she had finally met Toby Simpson, a new employee of her father's. Clever, polished and ambitious Toby. Desperate to feel normal and approved of, Annabel — with a little prompting from her mother — had convinced herself she needed a husband and had accepted Toby's convenient proposal.

The marriage had lasted only six months and Annabel had slunk out of it even less confident in herself than before. That had been nearly ten years ago and she was no longer a wimp. But men still stared, and to her profound irritation, she was still unnerved by it.

The next morning, in the overstated luxury of Swain Buddle Jessup, a whole herd of them stared.

Jessup, Senior introduced her to the gaping room. "My partners."

Buddle was short and solid like a pit bull. Annabel could just imagine him in court reducing some teenage rape victim to tears. Swain was clearly miscast as a lawyer — a Harvard Med School reject, she decided. Someone called Zimmerman who looked like Rambo in a suit was mauling his fountain pen as if it were a wrist iron. There were several others whose names she immediately forgot.

And then Jessup himself, a walking advertisement for hair transplants.

"We're all very pleased you could join us, Miss Worth," he began in a voice like glucose.

"Ms.," said Annabel coolly, wondering again what could possibly have warranted this conference.

He recovered quickly. "Ms. Worth." A slight bow in her direction.

The partners stared and Annabel resisted the urge to stretch her skirt further over her knees. She crossed her ankles instead and twisted her heavy gold signet ring.

"We felt it our duty to discuss in private with you the contents of your late aunt's will," Jessup intoned. "You are, after all, her principal beneficiary, apart from a handful of legacies to friends and charities." He waved a dismissive hand as though these stood for nothing, and Annabel frowned. They were acting as if all this was old news to her.

"As you are no doubt aware, your aunt's estate is considerable . . ." He coughed politely. The partners nodded and stared. Zimmerman inched forward in his seat and worked his legs as though jogging on the spot.

Annabel raised a hand. "Wait," she said bluntly. "Mr. Jessup, I have no idea what you are talking about."

At that the room broke up into murmurs and

everyone stared again, eyes glinting, like large rats sizing up their next meal.

"I don't think she knows," Buddle whispered audibly to Jessup.

"You are Miss ... Ms. Annabel Worth of Back Bay, Boston?" Jessup inquired belatedly.

Annabel nodded and smoothed a wayward strand of hair back into its French plait.

"Then we have some very good news for you," the lawyer declared with the smugness endemic to his profession.

Two hours later Annabel dragged off her clothes and collapsed onto her hotel bed. She still couldn't believe it. Aunt Annie had left her everything; and everything was, as Buddle had so succinctly put it, "one helluva lot for a little lady to manage on her own."

As she had prepared to leave, Jessup had produced two sealed envelopes, almost as an afterthought.

"Your aunt left these with me," he explained, escorting Annabel to the elevator. "One is for you." He passed her a pale lavender envelope. "The other is for someone called Lucy." He studied Annabel's face for a moment. "I wonder whether you know anyone going by that name, a friend of your aunt's perhaps, or a staff member?"

Annabel shrugged. "No I don't, Mr. Jessup."

"In that case we will need to make inquiries. Miss Adams gave us no other information." He slid the envelope back into his breast pocket with a resigned air. "If we are unable to trace this woman we will seek your instructions, Ms. Worth."

Whatever had possessed her aunt to deal with the likes of Jessup and his firm, she wondered now. From all accounts they did not have a single senior female partner and the thought of leaving everything in their hands was the stuff nightmares were made of. But Annabel didn't want to think about that right now.

Propping a couple of pillows behind her, she tore open her aunt's letter and read it once quickly then again very slowly. It was dated three months earlier.

My Dear Annabel,

By the time you read this, I will no doubt have met my maker and you will be wondering why you are my sole heir. As I write my body is exhausted from that wretched chemotherapy and I know I have little time.

For many years I have wanted to discuss with you certain matters of importance, but it now seems I haven't the strength.

The answers can be found on Moon Island.

Please go there as soon as you can and you will understand.

I wish you a happy life, my dear girl. Know that I have always loved you.

Annie

CHAPTER TWO

"Moon Island," Cody repeated.

The travel agent stabbed a long red nail at a dot on her map. "Gorgeous," she breathed. "Totally private. Just five houses on the whole place, and they're leased out only to women." She paused a little uncertainly then half-whispered, "An eccentricity of the owner's, I gather. Something to do with security ..." She trailed off, noting Cody's grey eyes widen.

"Women only," Cody repeated.

The agent did her best to look enthusiastic.

"Don't let that put you off," she gushed. "It's the kind of place you go to get away from it all, almost like a retreat. Most of my clients *adore* it. Why, just last week a lady dropped in to tell me she found it *absolutely* fabulous and didn't miss men a bit!"

"Imagine that," Cody said, deadpan. "As a matter of fact it sounds exactly the kind of thing I'm looking for."

"You won't regret it." The red fingernails fluttered over a reservation slip. "Expensive, but then in this business I always say you get what you pay for. Now, how many days was that?"

"A month," said Cody, producing her wallet and extracting a wad of notes. "And that's cash."

"Cash?" The agent froze, slightly bemused. "Cash money?" she squeaked as though she'd never seen the folding stuff.

Cody pushed the notes across the desk and watched her count them.

Earlier that day the bank had been pretty astounded too.

"You want to close your account and draw the full balance?" The teller had disappeared to get the floor manager, a grim-faced woman wearing a frilly shirt and a scarf covered in bank logos. She had escorted Cody into a private office where she explained that it would take some time to prepare such an amount. Was Cody sure she wanted it all at once?

"I'm leaving the country," Cody told her.

The woman smiled glacially. "We could prepare some travelers checks for you, Ms. Stanton," she offered. "In a hard currency. It would be much safer."

"Thank you," Cody said. "But I'd rather just have the cash." Travelers checks were too easily traced. "If you could let me have some in US dollars that would be handy."

The manager had eyed her with an expression close to pity. Poor creature, it said. She obviously had no idea, and traveling overseas, too, God help her.

Cody was told to return in an hour when the bank would provide her with the cash in a combination-locked briefcase with an optional wrist chain. Wearing a martyred expression, the floor manager had escorted her out.

Soon after, briefcase in hand, Cody had marched into the nearest travel agency with no idea where she should go. Somewhere very private, she had told the perfumed agent, somewhere obscure, inaccessible and beautiful.

Somewhere like New Zealand? the agent had joked, and for a moment Cody even considered the possibility. She could take a ferry to the South Island and vanish into the wilds of the West Coast, hole up in some gold-mining town along with every other crime escaping a police dragnet. She could change her name and become a guide on the whale-spotting boats in Kaikoura . . .

No, she decided, New Zealand was too small. Sooner or later she would phone home in a moment of weakness, or worse, bang into someone she knew and . . . curtains! They'd be onto her.

The sooner she left, the better. And on a one-way ticket so no one would know her ultimate destination. She had already given notice at her flat. All she needed to do now was say goodbye to her

Mother and she could camp at Janet's place until she left.

"You're going *where* and you want me to do *what?*" Cody's best friend Janet stared at her as though she had taken leave of her senses.

"I'm leaving New Zealand," Cody said. "I'll be staying on an island near Rarotonga. After that I'll probably head for London and pick up a job." She shoved the small black briefcase across the floor. "I want you to mind this while I'm away and I also want you to tell no one where I've gone. No one at all."

Janet pushed a stray brown curl out of her eyes and examined the locked bag with a dubious expression. "Looks like Fort Knox," she said. "What's in it, anyway?"

"Personal stuff," Cody told her blandly. "Papers, will and so on." That at least was true, she thought with a pang of guilt. There was also eighty thousand dollars in there, but she figured what Janet didn't know couldn't hurt her.

"Cody . . ." Her friend came over and squeezed her shoulders in a hug. "I know you're upset at the moment with breaking up with Margaret and losing your job and everything. But you won't do anything too hasty, will you?"

Cody leaned into Janet's arm and released a deep sigh. She felt like pouring out the whole story — what had really happened with Margaret, her job and the money, her escape plan — how everything felt so scary now that she was leaving tomorrow.

Instead she said throatily, "I'm gonna miss you like anything." That was also true. Janet was the kind of friend everyone hoped for. She was loyal, fun, and always there. Lovers could come and go, but Janet still made the best guacamole in town.

"I'll miss you too," Janet said. "You are coming back though, aren't you?" Her puppy-sad brown eyes combed Cody's face as though searching for more than a simple answer.

"I promise," Cody whispered, and hoped it was true.

≈ ≈ ≈ ≈ ≈

"You're doing *what!*" Nathaniel Kleist glowered at the tall blonde woman sitting opposite him.

"It's all there in writing, Nat." Annabel referred him to the single typewritten sheet on his blotter.

"I can read," he grunted, brushing the letter aside like a dead bug. "But I'm asking you what you're *really* doing? I mean for God's sake, Annabel, you're my best broker. If it's more money you're after, in Jesus' sweet name ask! If you don't like your new secretary just say so and I'll buy you another one."

He was on his feet, pacing the huge art-filled office like a caged bear. Drama queen — they'd invented the term for Nat.

"Nat," Annabel said with an air of finality. "My contract's up and I'm not coming back. For personal reasons. That's it. End of story."

"Personal reasons." He clutched his forehead and leaned heavily against his hand-painted Italian blinds. Then he fixed Annabel with an accusing look. "It's New York, isn't it? What are they offering?"

"Nat!" Annabel got to her feet. "Enough!" She started toward the door.

"I'll better it." He rushed after her. "I'll double it ... Annabel don't *do* this to me."

"Nat!" Annabel raised her voice. "I'm leaving. I'm giving up trading. There's no New York, no headhunters. I've resigned, that's all."

"It's a man!" He leaned against the door to prevent her opening it and suddenly grinned at her indulgently. "Why didn't you say so? You wanna stay at home and keep his slippers warm. Hey, not a problem ... we can hook you up, screen in the bedroom if you like ... you name it, sweetheart. Work from home."

"Nat, I'm flattered," Annabel lied. "But it isn't a man. It's something far more interesting than that."

"It is?" Nat frowned, clearly puzzled at the idea.

"It's an island," she enlightened him reluctantly. "I've inherited a Pacific island, if you must know, I'm going to go and live out there for a while."

Nat pulled the door open, his face a study in wan disbelief. "An island." He shook his head, and was muttering to himself as Annabel stepped past him. "Cracked," she heard him say. "Burnt out, poor kid."

CHAPTER THREE

The heat hit her like a blast furnace and Cody automatically started fanning herself with the unread paperback she had nursed for most of her eight-hour flight.

Trooping across the tarmac with a cluster of well-fed Kiwis in baggy pink shorts and florid cotton tops, she felt conspicuous in jeans and a long-sleeved checked shirt.

This is the tropics, she reminded herself belatedly, where civil servants let it all hang out and honeymoon couples travel on group discount. She paused at the customs entrance while round-faced local women dropped sweet-smelling leis over the heads of each passenger. A crew-cut German ordered his wife to photograph him, grinning, with an arm around an island woman. Cody flinched.

Customs and Immigration was a cursory affair. Name, destination, rubber stamp, have a nice day, next! They didn't bother with visas on the Cook Islands. You stayed thirty-one days, longer if you could pay.

Various bellhops and touts waving hotel signs were clustered at the main doors and Cody struggled to remember her travel agent's instructions. The tourists were dispersing, herded into all manner of transport including an extraordinary number of Subarus. Stragglers like Cody fiddled with their bags, looked at their watches and thumbed through their itineraries. Cody watched for a man waving a sign saying MOON ISLAND. "Don't worry if he's late," the agent had said. "Time doesn't mean much where you're headed."

Heat shimmered off the road and Cody's pores oozed in sympathy. She wished she could just strip off her clothes and lie under a tree somewhere. Back home in Wellington, a hot day was when you had to take off your sweatshirt and even then you'd stash it in the car just in case. On record as the windiest city in the world, Wellington was notorious for its rapid weather shifts — one minute warm and balmy, the next a hailstorm. Its population, fancying themselves politically sensitive, tried to keep quiet about welcoming the Greenhouse Effect. But some optimists were already planting banana palms.

Cody wondered when she'd see the place again. It

felt so weird having bought a one-way ticket out. How would she know when it was safe to return, anyway? She'd probably be picked up by Customs the second she got off the plane. She marveled that they hadn't found her already. Rarotonga was, after all, a New Zealand territory.

She stretched, rolled up her sleeves and pulled open a couple of buttons. Her head was aching from the flight and she slid tired fingers into her hair, smoothing it back off her forehead.

"Miss Stanton?"

Cody swung around. The first thing she saw was a battered handpainted sign that read MOON ISLAND, the second was a tall woman standing beyond it. She had white-blonde hair caught back in a fluorescent pink band, and skin so pale that Cody found herself gaping dumbly. An albino. She must be an albino. *Don't stare,* she ordered herself the way mothers reprimand children for pointing at cripples.

"Name's Mitchell." The voice came closer. It sounded very British. "Bevan Mitchell. I'm your pilot."

Cody refocused blankly on the sign and the man tucking it under one arm. He wore light cotton fatigues and a dilapidated straw hat. A cigarette drooped from a permanent groove in his bottom lip and a pair of aviators swung from his breast pocket.

"My pilot?" Cody repeated, subconsciously looking for a uniform.

"These your bags?" He picked them up before she could answer and told her, "Follow me."

Cody looked back across his shoulder. The woman had gone, she realized with a faint shock of disappointment. Perhaps she was never really there at all; a ghost or mere figment of her imagination brought on by the lethal combination of heat and stress.

She stumbled after the man and halted dumbstruck a few paces up the tarmac where their transport was parked. Cody watched with horror as he stowed her bags, and the body of the little biplane rattled and quivered. It was a four-seater twin-engine job. Postwar, but not by much. Cody shuddered at the sight of its delicately strutted wings with their thin silvery fabric cover. They were probably due to crumple from metal fatigue any time now, she thought gloomily.

The pilot was checking the propellers and called to her, "In you get, old girl."

"Crime doesn't pay," Cody muttered and hoisted herself up.

The interior was a battered shell crammed with parcels and boxes. She occupied one of the two dwarf-sized bucket seats in the back and wondered where to put her legs. A crate of bananas was on the floor between her seat and the pilot's. Gingerly she squeezed her feet down one side and twisted sideways in the rock-hard seat.

"Watch your head," she heard. A second passenger appeared in the doorway.

Astonished, Cody changed position again. It was her. The ghost. She quickly looked elsewhere. *Don't stare.*

"Belted in?" The pilot's head appeared in the hatch and Cody groped about for the ancient straps. It seemed a fairly pointless precaution given the circumstances, she thought. They were probably going to be killed anyway, that's if they ever got off the ground.

"Here, let me." A pair of hands interrupted her fumbling, clicked the belt shut and adjusted the strap length to fit across her lap snugly. Cody blushed at the bizarre intimacy of the action. It was totally innocent of course, a helpful gesture on the part of an experienced passenger. Cody's whole body tensed nonetheless.

"Thanks," she blurted with a nervous laugh.

"Have you flown much in smaller airplanes?" the ghost asked her conversationally. It was a low, slightly husky voice, with an accent that sounded American but hinted at England. She would sing divinely, Cody decided, and studied the speaker.

"No, as a matter of fact this is my first time," she admitted.

"Oh really?" The stranger took off her dark glasses and blinked into the harsh glare beyond the plane. "I guess there's a first time for everything," she added lightly. "And if memory serves me, it will probably turn out to be an anticlimax."

Cody felt her pulse leap. It was innuendo. No, it was nothing. She was confused. The cockpit was hot and airless, cramped and sticky. She'd recently broken up with her lover. She was sexually frustrated. She looked up and met the woman's eyes. *Don't stare.* They were extraordinary; bright pale blue, almost lavender, a subtle hint of pink in the irises. *Now you see it, now you don't.*

Cody looked away then looked back again. Her brows and lashes were dark, a shock against her absolute fairness. No doubt thanks to a beautician, she convinced herself. And what *was* that perfume? It was like nothing Cody had ever smelled, warm and delicious, a hint of vanilla and something else, one of those heady tropical flowers. They were sitting so close it was almost impossible to avoid breathing her in, and Cody wriggled in her seat.

"Are you nervous?" she was asked very softly.

"Yes," Cody said after a moment and she met the woman's eyes then quickly looked away, startled at what appeared to be a very definite bedroom stare.

The engines roared, or more accurately, coughed into life, and Cody was suddenly aware of a third person.

"Tally ho!" Their pilot screwed around to them with a cheerful grin. "Hold onto your hats, girls."

The din was awesome, the fumes nauseating. Breathe, Cody told herself as they bounced and spluttered up the runway. Her teeth were chattering and she felt thoroughly sick. This was madness, she decided as they gathered speed. She wished she could just give the money back and slink home. What on earth had possessed her to trade her nice safe routine existence for a life of crime? She could easily have got another job, and given time she'd get over Margaret.

Cody could almost hear her mother, *One day you're going to regret your impulsiveness, my girl, and I hope I'm there to see it.*

Look at me now, she wanted to shout. Instead she stole a look through the murky little window beside her and gasped, "We're up in the air!"

The other two laughed at her amazement.

"God's running a special on miracles this week," Bevan Mitchell called over his shoulder and it was as though the little De Havilland relaxed all of a sudden, completely at home in the wide sky. The shuddering died away and the dull thud of the propellers sounded reassuringly constant as they lolloped away from Rarotonga.

"Have you been to the island before?" the woman asked when sufficient time had passed to enable Cody to recover from the "anticlimax" of take-off.

She shook her head. "Have you?"

The woman nodded. "I'm staying there now." She wore her glasses again and Cody was ashamed to feel relief. Those lavender eyes were way too unnerving. "My name is Annabel, by the way. Annabel Worth."

"I'm Cody Stanton."

"Cody?" Annabel rolled the name about experimentally and Cody imagined hearing her whisper it, cry it as they . . .

Shocked, she banished the image. *Shame on you.* Her mother's voice. *And your sheets still warm from Margaret.*

"Cody, short for Cordelia," she explained, clearing her throat and dragging her eyes away from the woman's mouth.

She felt a hand brush her arm. "Look." Annabel pointed past their pilot. "There it is. Moon Island."

Cody caught a speck in the distance then closed her eyes and clutched her stomach as the tiny plane abruptly dropped a few hundred feet.

"Sorry about that," Bevan said cheerfully. "Just testing her reflexes."

"I think we can survive without the aerobatics today, Bevan," Annabel said with a familiarity that caused Cody's brow to pucker slightly.

These two obviously weren't strangers, she thought with a slight knot in her stomach. Were they lovers? She stole a look at Annabel and almost protested out loud at the idea. Irrational, of course. It was nothing to do with her whom this woman slept with. Typical though, she thought morosely. The first woman she'd fancied since the Margaret drama turns out to be straight. Very convenient, Cody told herself. It was always safer to lust after the unattainable, of course.

Swallowing a sigh, she peered boldly out her window as the plane banked to the right, and willed herself not to faint. The sea looked close, Van Gogh blue, and suitably shark-infested. The island ahead seemed almost mirage-like. It rose sweetly out of the ocean like a glimpse of paradise, and as they drew closer, Cody saw the glow of a coral reef beneath the water, a white beach curving around a thatch of palm trees. It was beautiful, breathtaking. And suddenly a reckless optimism chased the negative thoughts from her head. If such a place could exist on the same earth as cold, windy Wellington, surely anything was possible.

Bevan's voice intruded on her thoughts. "We're coming in now." They promptly lurched into a steep nosedive, the shuddering and rattling starting all over again.

"Don't worry," Annabel told her. "I do this most days and I'm still alive."

Cody tried to smile but her teeth were clenched. She clasped her hands together and refused to permit her life to flash before her. If she was about to be killed, at least she wanted to think about something cheerful.

"We're nearly there," the soft voice said. "That's Passion Bay beneath us."

Cody felt warm breath on her cheek, smelled that impossible fragrance. Her eyes flicked open and she peeped past the pilot. Passion Bay. Palm trees. All she could see was palm trees. The plane seemed to stall then, dropping out of the sky like a slaughtered bird.

"Oh God," Cody whispered, falling back on the patriarchy now that the chips were down. There was a pronounced thud and she held onto her seat as they swayed and jolted to a merciful standstill.

As soon as Bevan Mitchell gave the okay, Annabel opened the hatch and sprang lithely to the ground, but Cody's legs were trembling so much she didn't think she could move. After an embarrassingly long pause, during which she pretended to fumble about for her satchel while her shattered nerves regrouped, Cody descended awkwardly.

"Well then." Annabel turned, hands on hips, and smiled at her full blast. "How was that for you?"

Leaning back against a wing, Cody opened her eyes. Innuendo again. Lesbian innuendo? Or was it all wishful thinking? Maybe Annabel and the pilot *were* just friends. But she could still be straight. She was probably married. Married and bored.

Cody sized her up. She wore a pink T-shirt and baggy knee-length white shorts. Her body was athletic, muscles clearly defined. Aerobics, Cody decided; her face was free of that slightly harassed expression joggers wore.

She was waiting for a reply and Cody wondered what her eyes were asking behind those all-concealing lenses. "For me?" Cody very deliberately ran her tongue across her lips and casually flicked open the next few buttons of her shirt. "I guess you could say the earth moved."

Cody grinned and imagined the stranger naked, hot; imagined sliding against her, stroking her hair. This time she let herself fantasize.

CHAPTER FOUR

Monday.
I am tired. Unbelievably tired. It breaks my heart to say goodbye to my beautiful island. I planted another hibiscus near Rebecca's frangipani tree this morning and made my farewells. My body aches. I cannot endure another needle. They tell me I'm a fool to refuse further treatment but I'll swear it's worse than the disease. I can't turn away their pain relief, though. Since it went into my

bones I simply can't imagine how a person does without the drugs. Last night I dreamed of Rebecca, dreamed she was holding me again. I am nearly ready to leave and still I have not written to Annabel . . .

Guiltily Annabel snapped her aunt's diary closed. The answer is on the island, the letter had said. Surely she didn't have to invade her aunt's privacy, snoop about among the most intimate details of another woman's life to uncover it. Was that what Aunt Annie had intended?

For a moment Annabel imagined someone else in her shoes, some cousin who had barely known Annie. What would they make of the diaries? Over thirty years worth piled into boxes in her aunt's attic study. And the letters! Bundle after bundle, tied with thin ribbon and stuffed into the window seat.

The house itself was wonderful, a large sprawling timber construction, skirted all around with deep shady verandahs and opening into a central garden-filled courtyard. Its name was Villa Luna and Annabel had loved it at first sight. It was built on the highest northwestern aspect of the island and looked out across jungle and palms to the huge blue of the Pacific.

Exploring the property, Annabel had been amazed and delighted at how immediately at home she felt there, how oddly familiar it all seemed. It was as though she belonged, as though in some strange way the island had been waiting for her.

At the back of the villa was a small grassy area

and a stable housing a single black mare. Aunt Annie had adored horses and Kahlo, as the mare was called, had arrived by ferry only last year after her predecessor had died of old age. *I can't ride her,* Annie had noted in her diary, *But I can watch her run and keep her company.* According to Mrs. Marsters, who kept house for the island two days a week, the mare had often been tethered to the verandah and Annie would sit reading and writing, periodically talking to the horse like a friend.

During her first week on the island, Annabel had gradually befriended the elegant creature, and today for the first time she saddled her up. Kahlo shied a little initially, then whickered her acceptance as Annabel climbed into the saddle and gently reined her toward the jungle tracks. Soon Kahlo was behaving as though she had never known another rider. Her tail lifted, she stretched her pace, and responded to Annabel's commands like a showjumper.

She guided the mare down to Passion Bay and trotted along the beach, careful not to overtire the horse after her more sedentary existence. Later in the afternoon she tethered her to the front verandah and was gratified when the mare approached and contentedly nuzzled her lap while she read.

The diary was dated 1956.

Father is at me again to marry Roger and even Laura is hounding me. I just don't know what to do. I've told Rebecca that I must see her and begged her to come with me this summer. She says I cannot dither any longer and I must put poor Roger out of his misery, but he refuses to listen. What can I do?

Three weeks later another passage:

Oh joy, Oh bliss. Rebecca is coming with me to Europe. Last night we sat for hours in her car just talking and Rebecca gave me this little ring with a diamond horseshoe set in it for luck. I can hardly concentrate for thinking about her, imagining her on some Greek Island, wearing only flowers.

Annabel closed her eyes and stroked Kahlo absently. She had known Annie was a lesbian, her mother's scandalous younger sister, the family skeleton in the closet. But who was Rebecca? Her aunt had never mentioned her. Yet obviously they had been in love, perhaps even lovers. In 1956.

She sipped her lime soda and lapsed for a moment into her own private fantasy. The woman on the plane yesterday brought it on. Cody. Short for Cordelia. Annabel remembered her deep, lazy accent. Australian-sounding, only softer. *I lahve swemming,* she'd said, looking down at the sea. And Annabel remembered; New Zealand was an island too.

Cody had seemed very nervous, had avoided looking at her directly. Did she find her repulsive? Annabel wondered with the same kind of pang she'd experienced all through adolescence. She could have sworn she'd caught a look of genuine interest, and had flirted lightly to test the water. Cody had responded; she hadn't imagined that.

Cody was in Hibiscus Villa, the house nearest hers. Peering, Annabel made out in the distance the pattern of a thatched roof. Perhaps she would call in on some pretext in a few days, she decided. Maybe invite her to dinner.

She conjured up a picture of Cody sitting on her verandah, smoothing back that dark cropped hair with the same appealing gesture that had caught her eye at the airport. Annabel found herself wondering when she had last made love. A year ago? Longer? She could hardly remember. She didn't have the time or energy these days it seemed. But suddenly she wanted to change all that. Warm, perfumed air, Annabel decided, went straight to the groin.

æ æ æ æ æ

Cody pulled off her shorts and left them in a heap with her shirt, hat and shades on the beach. It was stupid to wear togs, she supposed, on an empty beach with no one to shock but a few gulls. But old habits died hard and Cody had never been nude bathing in her life.

She poked an experimental toe into the water. It was clear and very warm. Reveling in its balmy touch, she swam out into the lagoon, conscious of the outlying coral reef and testing the currents for safety.

The water was amazingly calm, totally different from the chilly surf she was used to in Wellington. It was almost too good to be true, she decided, flipping onto her back and drifting toward the shore. Back home everyone would be shivering in their woollen pants, lighting fires and buying king-size boxes of tissues. And here she was, swanning about on a deserted island, lapping up the sun and sea on a beach called, of all things, Passion Bay.

How did it get its name? she wondered idly, and imagined a range of highly erotic possibilities, most of them involving the woman on the plane. *Annabel.* Cody tested the name silently and remembered her bedroom smile, the way she had stood, hands on hips, eyeing Cody. The way she had flirted.

She seemed very sophisticated, quite unlike anyone Cody knew. She thought of Margaret then . . . small voluptuous Margaret, the life and soul of the party, the woman who could sell sand to the Arabs. Her throat tightened and she fought off a flood of memories.

Damn Margaret! Cody wished she could erase every trace of her from her life, slam the door on the last five years. She wished she could forget that Margaret's favorite color was blue, the very same blue as the sky over Passion Bay. She wished she could forget her face, the dark little freckles across her nose, her innocent teasing eyes. But somehow Margaret just kept seeping in through the smallest cracks in her consciousness, at the very moments when Cody least expected her.

She felt sand and hoisted herself up the beach as a half-hearted breaker lapped over her. To hell with Margaret. This was her holiday and she was not about to let thoughts of her ex-lover dominate it. Margaret had done enough damage already. Willing herself to relax and empty her mind, Cody squirmed decadently in the warm grains and shielded her eyes from the glare.

"I hope you're wearing a sun block," a voice intruded just as she felt herself nodding off. Startled, she blinked up at the speaker. It was *her*, this time staring down with an expression of faint concern.

"You're probably not used to this kind of heat," she told Cody in a businesslike tone. "Although I guess you don't need to be as careful as I do."

Annabel wore a white pajama-style outfit in lightweight cotton and a large drooped-brim hat. Her skin was so fair she would burn terribly unless she protected it Cody figured. If Annabel ever sported a tan it would be compliments of Clarins.

"I thought you might have fallen asleep," Annabel went on. "And I was worried."

Cody pulled herself up to sitting position, at once conscious of her inadequate bikini top and Annabel's steady lavender gaze. "I am using cream," she told Annabel. "And I do tan easily. But you're right. Even with my skin I'd turn to lobster if I lay out here all afternoon."

Annabel lowered herself onto the sand next to Cody. Cody felt suddenly tongue-tied.

"I plaster myself all over in factor forty. I'm always terrified I'll miss a spot so I tend to keep my clothes on." Annabel stretched, propped herself back on her hands and surveyed Cody with open interest. "How's the water?"

"It's divine," Cody enthused. "Beats a sand storm on Lyall Bay any day."

Annabel looked sideways at Cody. "Lyall Bay?"

"A beach where I live. The place is more famous for its wind than its surf. Open your mouth and it fills up with sand."

Annabel laughed softly. It melted like caramel in the back of her throat. "Sounds like a real resort."

Cody nodded. "It can be at times. That's when the locals aren't tossing fish and chip wrappers all over it and letting their rottweilers practice guard duty on the swimmers."

Annabel's eyes sparkled and Cody rolled onto one elbow to face her. "What do you do for a job?"

Annabel didn't answer at first. She extracted a pair of dark glasses from her pocket and quickly slid them on. "At the moment I'm not working," she said. It sounded a little evasive and Cody wondered with a sudden jolt whether she'd lost her job too.

"Me neither," Cody told her. "I was made redundant."

"Redundant? Oh, you mean laid off." Annabel slid onto her back and Cody watched the soft cotton shirt settle on the outline of her breasts. She wasn't wearing a bra and the fabric clung slightly where her skin was damp with the heat. Cody experienced a crazy urge to lean across and bite a nipple softly through the thin covering. Embarrassed, she looked away.

"What was your job?" Annabel asked.

"I'm a DBA," Cody replied. "Database Administrator."

"Computers." Annabel sounded dismayed. "Wonderful inventions, but ..."

"Who'd want to work with them?" Cody finished for her.

Annabel smiled quickly. "I'm sorry. I hope you're not offended."

"Deeply," Cody said poker-faced. "You've no idea what it does to a girl's social life to talk computers — I mean women are simply bowled right over, rendered speechless." She sat up and brushed the sand slowly off her arms and breasts and began to apply more lotion in long slow caresses, conscious of Annabel's eyes following her movements.

Cody dropped her voice conspiratorially. "It's the mystique of the machine." She turned her attention to her legs, parting them to rub the cream along the insides of her thighs. "Why do you do it, they ask ..." She paused, dropped the bottle in front of Annabel, and removed her bikini top, saying, "Would you mind doing my back?"

Annabel squeezed some warm oil into her palm and stroked it into Cody's shoulders. "So why do you do it?" she asked.

"Because it's there," Cody said blandly. Annabel burst out laughing. "Well thank you for sharing," she said, as Cody replaced her bikini top. "Seriously though, aren't there things you'd rather be doing?"

Cody shrugged. "I can't think of anything." She heard the trace of defensiveness in her own voice.

Annabel moved a little closer. "Are you sure about that?" she asked softly. She moistened her top lip with the tip of her tongue.

Innuendo, Cody was thinking, definite innuendo. She had been flirting with Annabel and the other woman was returning it in kind. But then perhaps Annabel flirted with everyone, female or male. Some women got so used to sexual game-playing that it became unconscious. Well two could play at that, and Cody was a free woman now. She could do what she liked.

She returned Annabel's look candidly. "That would depend on what was offered."

As Annabel removed her glasses and sat forward, clasping her arms around her knees, Cody changed to a more conversational tack. "So how do you like the island?"

"I love it here. After Boston it's just so tranquil. The air tastes really fresh and everything is so ... so tropical. Have you ever been to Boston, Cody?"

"I've never visited the States at all," Cody confessed. "Back home most people think it's really dangerous. You know, crime everywhere, lunatics shooting up McDonalds, crack kids. That's all we get to hear about in the news."

"And all I know about New Zealand is that you have the most sheep in the world."

"That's right," Cody told her. "Three million people and seventy million sheep. Sometimes it's hard to tell the difference."

Annabel laughed. It was deep rich laughter which lingered in the warm air about them. "I guess vegetarianism is virtually a capital offense, then."

Cody grinned. "No," she said. "We're all very biodegradable. Besides, we don't have to eat our mutton, we sell it to the Iranians."

"You *talk* to the Iranians?"

"No," Cody said placidly. "We sell to them."

Both women chuckled. "Are you married?" Annabel asked abruptly.

"Good God no!" Cody gave a graphic shudder,

then felt embarrassed that she might have given offense. Guardedly, she asked Annabel, "Are you?"

"I was once," Annabel said. "Years ago in my callow youth."

Cody felt a sharp pang of disappointment. Annabel was straight after all. Or was she? Heaps of lesbians had been married. "So what happened?"

"I guess what didn't happen was more to the point," Annabel replied. "I was just a kid and Toby was everything my parents hoped for. I had such low self-esteem back then that I would have done nearly anything for approval ..."

Low self-esteem! Cody's face must have registered her disbelief, because Annabel looked suddenly defensive. "I know it's probably hard for someone like you to understand," she said. "You seem so confident. I suppose you've never had any doubts about yourself."

What did she mean by that? Cody wondered. Doubts about being a lesbian? "To a certain extent that's true, Annabel," she admitted. "But I wouldn't say I'm brimming with self-esteem. Especially since ..." She trailed off and deftly changed the subject. "So anyway what happened to Mr. Terrific?"

"I left him after six months. Told him he deserved better than a frigid wife."

Cody snorted. "I guess there was no question that you were the one with the problem?"

Annabel shook her head. "It was the quickest way out. Besides, I'd fallen for someone else, and it didn't feel a bit like how it was with Toby."

Cody raised interested eyes and urged, "Do tell, this is better than *Days of Our Lives*."

"It was a woman," Annabel said quietly. "Miss Clarice Harvey, my mother's new piano teacher. She was wonderful. Tall, clever and very pre-Raphaelite. I'd moved back home after my marriage broke up and she used to visit once a week. After three months I asked her out." She fell into reflective silence.

Cody prompted, "Did she accept?"

"Yes," Annabel sighed. "But I'm afraid it was unrequited lust all the way. She was engaged to a violinist with the Boston Symphony and she wanted to bring him along on our date."

"Say no more." Cody grimaced. "Did you let her?"

"Of course not," Annabel said. "But she spent the whole evening talking about him anyway. God it was a disaster! In the end I bared my soul and, as calm as you please, she said, *Oh my goodness you must be a lesbian.*"

Cody burst out laughing then apologized. "Hell, I'm sorry. Talk about insensitive . . ."

"Don't worry about it," Annabel said. "I've always aspired to comedy. Anyway, do *you* know anyone who has a nice straightforward coming out story?"

"Well actually . . ." Cody grinned as Annabel rolled her eyes.

"You *don't.*"

" 'Fraid so," Cody said. "I just started falling in love with girls and finally one of them loved me back."

"You've never dated guys?"

"A few times," Cody admitted. "Double dates mostly. But nothing serious, I mean I've never slept with one or anything."

"Lucky you," Annabel muttered, then looked at

Cody closely. "So are you in a relationship at the moment?"

Cody paused, looked away, and bit her lip slightly. "No, not at the moment," she finally responded and her throat felt tight. "I recently ..." she began, but Annabel touched her arm lightly, unexpectedly.

"I'm sorry," she said. "When did it happen?"

"Five weeks ago," Cody said flatly and cradled her head against her knees for a moment.

Annabel stroked Cody's arm tentatively. "Been pretty rough?"

Cody nodded, hunching her shoulders. She wished she didn't feel so raw still. Here she was in this beautiful place with this beautiful woman and what was she doing? Talking about her ex.

"Is that why you came to the Island?" Annabel was asking.

"That's part of the reason," she admitted huskily.

"And the rest?" Annabel's hand had moved around to rest lightly on Cody's shoulders and Cody leaned gratefully into the warmth of it.

"It's very complicated," she said evasively.

"I'm sorry. You must think me dreadfully inquisitive. I don't mean to be."

Cody looked up at her, smiled and shrugged. "It's okay," she said. "I just find it hard to talk about, that's all. I guess I need to do some 'work' on my grief."

Annabel grinned. "How about doing some work on your holiday instead, and having dinner with me tonight?"

Cody felt her heart lurch. "Dinner?" she echoed. "That would be great."

"You're on then." Annabel started tracing a map in the sand with her finger. "This is where my place is," she explained. "Come around anytime. If I'm not there just grab a chair and help yourself to a drink." She got to her feet and brushed herself off. "I'm flying into Rarotonga this afternoon. Do you need anything?"

"No thanks," Cody said, and with a brief wave her companion strolled off across the white sand.

Annabel's house was very large and homely, not the least bit like a holiday place. It was full of books, ornaments and pictures and the wooden furniture looked old and loved.

"Do you actually live here all the time?" Cody asked, glancing about at the worn Persian rugs and huge potted palms.

"No, but my aunt does . . . did."

"Is your aunt . . ."

"Dead," Annabel completed flatly. "Yes, she died three weeks ago."

"I'm sorry. Were you very close?"

"Yes, later in her life we were. She left me this house," she said simply. "Can I get you another drink?" she offered.

"I'd better not. Champagne goes straight to my head." And besides, Cody had noticed that Annabel had barely touched her own glass. She allowed her gaze to drift across the woman at the other end of the sofa.

Annabel wore a white shirt tucked into faded old Levis and her hair was pulled back tightly into a French plait, an effective mixture of casual and formal which suited her perfectly.

"Have you always lived in Boston?" Cody asked.

The bright lavender eyes lifted. "Pretty much. I once made a bid to break out. I told my parents I was going to college at the University of California in Berkeley. That was in the seventies and you would have thought I'd just taken shares in Sodom and Gomorrah. Mother had a migraine for a week. Anyway it was short-lived and I ended up at Radcliffe where they could keep an eye on me. I was a real wimp back then."

"I find that hard to believe," Cody said. "Aren't you being a little hard on yourself?"

Annabel shrugged. "Sometimes I get frustrated when I look back. It feels like such a waste of time and I just can't believe how stupid I was."

"Do you mean not realizing you were a lesbian sooner?"

"I suppose so." Annabel said. "But also stuff about my appearance." She gazed at her hands reflectively. "I've always thought I was ugly. It doesn't seem to matter what anyone says, I still get paranoid at times."

"But you're stunning," Cody blurted. "I've never seen anyone quite like you." Her gaze rested on Annabel's mouth for a moment too long.

"I wasn't fishing for compliments," Annabel said a little stiffly.

Cody felt embarrassed. "I meant what I said,

Annabel. I think you're very beautiful." Blushing, she broke off and recklessly poured herself another glass of champagne.

There was only one way a conversation like this could end up, Cody realized, wishing suddenly that it had never begun. She hated playing games. It all seemed so farcical. Either she was going to bed with Annabel or she wasn't. And if she wasn't, it was time to leave — only she didn't want to yet. Draining her glass, she looked across at Annabel.

Something of her confusion must have showed. Annabel smiled slowly, poured her yet another champagne and relaxed back in her corner watching Cody lazily. She seemed very much in control and her slightly predatory expression made Cody nervous. After this drink she would leave, Cody decided. She gulped another large mouthful of the fruity liquid, letting the bubbles pinprick their way into her senses.

"This is wonderful," she said, staring into her glass, suddenly engrossed in the effervescence. Then to her horror she giggled as a warm rush rendered her legs weak and powerless.

"Oh dear," she murmured and hastily put her glass down, attempting to gather her scattering wits. She seldom drank alcohol, having learned the hard way that she made her worst mistakes after a few drinks. She thought about Margaret and how tempting it had been to head for a bar and stay there, obliterating the feelings. *It's Margaret who needs the lobotomy, not you*, a friend had said.

Cody yawned and then wondered what time it

was. She felt as though she'd only been with Annabel for a short while. The meal had been wonderful and their conversation easy and comfortable. Until now.

"You must be tired," Annabel interrupted her thoughts softly. "Would you like to lie down for a few minutes?"

Cody nodded and even as she did so she thought, *I don't believe this.* It was the oldest trick in the book and here she was falling for it hook, line and sinker. But she still allowed herself to be led into a dimly lit room and guided toward a large Futon bed. There were candles around the walls and their golden halos blurred and danced before her eyes.

"Annabel . . ." she began, but a finger was placed on her lips and the other woman pulled her down to sit on the edge of the bed.

"Relax, Cody." Annabel slid her fingers up into Cody's hair and around to massage the back of her neck. "You're very tense," she commented, probing the stiff tendons.

Cody nodded and reached up to touch Annabel's cheek with a tentative hand.

"Are you nervous?" Annabel asked.

Cody nodded again, wishing she could think of something quick and sophisticated to say. Annabel's fingers were kneading the tight muscles around her shoulders in a hypnotic rhythm. It felt delicious and Cody slid an arm around Annabel's waist and turned to face her.

In the haze of the candlelight, she looked soft and golden, like a goddess strayed to earth. Cody reached up, touched her hair. Like a web it clung to her fingers and she pulled out the pins, letting it spill down over Annabel's shoulders.

Cody was aware of her T-shirt being eased out of her jeans, of Annabel's hands caressing her back, drawing her closer. Her stomach hollowed and goosebumps crept across her flesh where Annabel explored. She closed her eyes and her head spun. She wanted to say something but the words wouldn't form. *You're drunk,* a distant voice reminded her.

Annabel was lowering her onto the bed and Cody did not resist. She felt a mouth on her neck, her shoulders, her breasts, and savored the sensations. When her T-shirt was slipped over her head, she opened her eyes and focused dazedly on her surroundings.

This was not her room, she thought foggily. The hands stroking her were not Margaret's. She stared up at Annabel and fell short of breath. Almost of their own accord, her muscles tensed. Annabel, this was Annabel. A woman she had only met two days ago. They were here in her room making love. This was not Margaret.

Cody's eyes stung suddenly and her lips began to tremble. Then she pushed her hands against Annabel and elbowed herself back into sitting position, head spinning.

This was not how she wanted it to be. She wanted ... she didn't know what she wanted.

"I can't," she stammered jerkily. Annabel drew back. Cody wet her lips and avoided Annabel's eyes.

"I just can't do this," she said miserably and lowered her head. "I'm sorry."

Annabel caught Cody gently against her. "No, *I'm* sorry, Cody," she said after a moment. "I guess I was taking a lot for granted." She touched Cody's cheek with her free hand, tilting her head up.

Cody was embarrassed. Her eyes were full of tears and her mouth was trembling. Somewhere inside a voice was persecuting her. *Fool, you want her don't you? What's the matter with you. Quit that whimpering.*

"It's just too soon, isn't it?" Annabel trailed a finger down Cody's wet cheek then licked the tears off it.

Cody nodded. "I feel like an idiot," she said bitterly. "It's been a month now and I just don't seem to be getting over her at all. I can hardly think of her without crying and I can hardly think of anything else but her!" She leaned forward, permitting Annabel to hold her, aware of the comfort of having her head stroked.

"What's her name?" Annabel asked quietly.

"Margaret," Cody said into her shoulder.

"You want to tell me about her?"

Cody turned her head, one cheek cushioned against Annabel's breasts. She could hear the regular thud of her heart and smell that familiar scent — vanilla, but not quite.

"I met her on a holiday job in my final year at University." Cody closed her eyes. "Strawberry picking. It was so hot and everything was sort of sticky and juicy. I had this enormous bucketful ready to weigh and she was lugging hers up to the station. My bucket wasn't where it should have been and she tripped over it." Cody chuckled softly. "There were strawberries everywhere."

"Very kinky," Annabel remarked lightly. "And what then?"

"We had this huge fight . . . a physical fight, and well . . . we both got the sack."

"Obviously a match made in heaven."

Cody grinned. "We started going out and a few months later we moved in together. That was nearly five years ago."

"Five years," Annabel raised her eyebrows. "You really were married then." She paused. "What happened, Cody?"

Cody braced herself. Every time she tried to say the words they eluded her, froze on her lips like little stones. She hadn't even been able to tell Janet, her best friend.

Annabel had pulled back slightly and was watching her. "You don't have to tell me, Cody," she said. "It just might help if you did, that's all."

Cody met her eyes and saw in them only warmth and genuine caring. No games.

"She left me," she said quietly. "There was . . ." A pause. "Someone else." The tears started again and Cody didn't bother to wipe them away. "It happened so fast. One minute we were lovers and the next she was saying how she'd never felt truly happy with me and it was all over. She had met this person and they were soul mates."

I have to leave you Cody, had been her exact

words, *I'd like us to stay friends but I'll understand if you can't. I still really care about you Cody.*

"Did you know the other woman?" Annabel asked.

Hunching her shoulders, Cody shook her head. "It was a man," she heard herself say, suddenly aware of nausea rising.

"A man ..." Annabel repeated blankly.

"I think I'm going to be sick," Cody told her. "I'll go to my place to do it."

CHAPTER FIVE

Cody rolled on her stomach and opened her paperback at page twenty-one which she had already read several times. The words ran together and she pulled off her Ray Bans, wiping the tiny beads of perspiration off the lenses with her T-shirt.

The alleyway was empty save for a mangy cat trying its luck in the garbage outside a cheap pasta joint. Amanda pressed her back flat against the grimy stone wall and inched her way along, one hand straying to the reassuring bulge of her Smith & Wesson.

Cody lifted the book up, shook out the sand, and tried to remember how Amanda came to be stroking a pistol in that dark alley. She back-tracked to the beginning of the chapter and skimmed a couple of pages, then dropped the book in disgust. She'd been trying to read it for days. Ever since that evening at Annabel's, in fact. So much for escapism, she thought miserably and rolled over to stare up at the palm trees.

The sky was a cloudless big-screen blue and the ocean pounded the reef with all the involuntary passion of a heartbeat. A slight breeze stirred the drooping palm fronds but just fell short of cooling the afternoon air.

A week, she'd been on the island for a week and she was homesick already. Cody conjured up a vision of her office, terminals banked up around the walls, printers spooling frantically. Suzie Wentworth concealing a cigarette behind the latest BYTE magazine. While she was there she'd hated it, but now that she couldn't return she missed the security and predictability of it all.

Marooned on a desert island . . . no ticket home. Why had she burnt her own boats, set herself up? If she hadn't kept the money, she could still have paid for her holiday and she could just fly home when it was all over, get a nice well-paid job, go to the movies with her friends, cruise the women's dances . . .

She hadn't spoken to Margaret before she left,

Cody remembered with a sharp pang. Maybe she would never speak to her again. And she'd given Janet explicit instructions to tell no one her address, not even Margaret.

"But what if she wants to talk?" Janet had protested. "Sometimes couples make up, Cody ... get back together." Janet was like that, eternally hopeful, anything for a happy ending.

"She won't be back," Cody had said with grim confidence. This was real life, not the movies.

What was Margaret doing now, she wondered. Jumping out of bed the second her alarm rang, pulling on her tracksuit and heading off for her morning run? Or was she living with what's-his-name already — cooking his dinners, washing his shirts? Cody pushed the horrible fragments of a memory out of her consciousness — Margaret sitting in the car with him after moving her furniture out, reaching across, kissing him ...

Rage crowded her, forcing her up off the sand and chasing her along the beach. "Bitch!" Cody shouted into the breakers. "Lousy, rotten bitch!"

Loud sobs forced their way out and she collapsed onto her knees weeping into the water's edge. Cody had no idea how long she stayed there, tears merging with the salt water until there was no distinguishing between them. It was the noise that first penetrated, a dull drumming as regular as the waves, only a different tempo. She looked up, saw nothing, listened again.

It wasn't the mercy mission, as Annabel jokingly referred to her regular flights in Bevan Mitchell's

Dominie. There was no whine, no screaming of displaced gulls as the little plane evicted the competition from its landing strip.

Cody wiped her face and got to her feet. It might have been a boat; maybe one of the other guests on the island was out fishing. She hadn't seen anyone else since she arrived, but Annabel had mentioned that there were three women staying on the other side of the island. She couldn't hear it anymore.

Shrugging, she returned to her beach towel and page twenty-one of her thriller. She found the mangy cat then stopped reading. There it was again, that soft rapid thrum. She sat up and scanned the beach to either side.

It was a horse, a black horse. Cody lowered her book. It was Annabel. She could vaguely remember her mentioning the animal now, and she wondered how it had got to the island in the first place. Horse and rider were approaching at a canter. With a frown, Cody contemplated her belongings.

She didn't want to see Annabel today, she thought, recalling the other night with a mixture of confusion and embarrassment. All Cody could remember was apologizing over and over, staggering along the jungle track with Annabel's stoic assistance, then rudely pushing her away when she offered to help her undress for bed. The next morning she had heard a knock at her door and, knowing it was Annabel, she had ignored it.

She was behaving badly, Cody realized. There was no need for her to avoid Annabel. They were both adults; they could talk this through like mature women. And besides, there was nothing to talk about. After all, nothing had happened. Cody could apologize for getting drunk and spoiling the evening, and Annabel . . .

Cody's gaze returned to the rider. If Cody hadn't stopped them, they would have made love. A one-night stand. Was that what Annabel wanted? A good time; sun, surf and sex?

What was wrong with that, Cody reasoned. Since when had she joined the Moral Majority anyway? With a defiant shrug she stuffed her towel and paperback into her bag and dusted the sand off her arms and legs. She would talk to Annabel, but not today. Dragging her feet a little, she retreated into the jungle beyond the palm trees.

꺙 꺙 꺙 꺙 꺙

Annabel dug her heels into Kahlo and felt the mare respond instantly. In the distance she had caught a glimpse of a dark head and something colorful, a towel perhaps. Cody. Part of her wanted to rush after her, part of her wanted to pretend she wasn't there. Pulling back on the reins, Annabel slowed the mare to a trot and watched Cody disappear.

She hadn't stopped kicking herself since that night. What on earth had got into her, plying the woman with champagne, assuming they would go to bed together, as though having sex was about as significant as coffee after dinner. No wonder Cody was avoiding her like the plague.

Annabel felt unwelcome butterflies invade her

stomach as visions of Cody flooded her mind. It had been months, years in fact, since she had wanted a woman so badly. She had almost forgotten what plain, old-fashioned lust felt like. Since she had started stock trading it was as though nothing else could compete with the adrenalin highs of her job. She had moved to the trading floor after her split with Clare and she had sworn then that it was the last time she would get "involved."

In retrospect, their relationship had been doomed from the start. Clare the out lesbian, the political activist; Annabel the privileged only child. They had fought as passionately as they loved and made love. They had talked around their differences for three years until what was unsaid became louder than words.

Annabel could never forget the leaving, holding each other and crying for what they would both be losing. Neither of them had been capable of articulating the feelings. Words had become traps, weapons, and could be trusted no longer. They had tried couples-counseling, but Clare considered therapy a middle-class soft option and Annabel had blamed their subsequent break-up on her unwillingness to participate.

They still wrote. Three times a year — on each other's birthdays and at Christmas. Since Clare there had been other women of course, but over the past year Annabel had found herself becoming less and less interested. Not long before Aunt Annie died it had even reached the stage where she began to wonder whether she was going straight.

It was on the island that she had started to have

some understanding of how soul-destroying her job was, how empty her life. She could finally admit that she was suffering physical withdrawal from the adrenalin highs her body had grown accustomed to — the alcohol, the caffeine.

Up till now Annabel hadn't put the pieces together. She hadn't wanted to, she supposed. But here, listening to the sea and breathing in fresh untainted air, she had started to think about her gradual weight loss, the periods missed, her ten cups a day coffee habit, her increasing social isolation and the exhaustion that knocked her sideways an hour after she finished work every night.

Why hadn't she seen it before? Some of her friends had, and Annabel recalled her hostile reactions with shock and remorse. She hadn't been ready to hear about it back then.

Guiding Kahlo into the jungle, Annabel located the route to Hibiscus Villa, paused, then reined the mare in the opposite direction. She wanted to see Cody. But it could wait.

I cannot believe how much has happened in one short year. I am engaged to Roger. My beloved Rebecca is still in London and Laura has married that pompous bore Theodore Worth ...

Laura and Theodore. Her parents. Annabel smiled at Aunt Annie's description of her father. There was no love lost between them. She flicked along a few pages.

I miss Rebecca desperately and write nearly every day. Her letters are full of some woman called Alexandra. They traveled to Paris together. I cannot bear to think of it but I know it is madness to feel such jealousy for one's best friend. Roger pesters me constantly to allow liberties but I simply loathe his hands all over me. I don't know how I will endure married life.

Annabel's brow creased. As far as she knew, Aunt Annie had never been married. She returned 1957 to its shelf and extracted the next volume. A wafer-thin letter slid out as she opened it. Annabel read the contents guiltily, feeling like a clumsy intruder on someone else's private world.

Sweet Annie,
I'm coming home and I shall never leave you again. I can't tell you how I feel knowing that you have finally accepted what we've always known in our hearts. Don't worry about Roger. He'll find some other girl and forget you soon enough. I'm so impatient to see you my darling. I want to take you in my arms and keep you there forever.

All my love,
Rebecca

Annabel refolded the letter and tucked it into the diary. She had an uncanny sense of not being alone, of someone else's presence in the house. For a second she wondered fancifully if it were her aunt's ghost, or maybe the unknown Rebecca.

Sliding the diary back into its place, she listened carefully but heard only the familiar waves on the distant reef, the rustle of palms, insect operatics.

"Is someone there?" She poked her head around the door of the upstairs attic and listened again. Footsteps. "Is that you Mrs. Marsters?"

"It's me," a voice responded from the verandah.

Annabel recognized the accent with a quickening of her pulse. "Cody?"

She descended the stairs and hurried out, suddenly conscious of her clothes, tiny cutoff shorts, a tatty old halter top. Her hair was loose and tangled from an afternoon catnap and she pushed it off her face with fingers that trembled slightly.

Cody was waiting on the verandah and Annabel's heart lurched at the sight of her. She was wearing a short brightly colored sarong knotted at the valley between her breasts. The knowledge that she wore nothing underneath affected Annabel in all sorts of ways, making her shorts decidedly uncomfortable and her breathing erratic. Cody was looking awkward, transferring her weight from one foot to the other as if she might bolt at a loud noise. What had she come for? To tell Annabel she was leaving the island or just to slap her face?

"Hi." She greeted Annabel with a quick uncertain smile as she stroked her hair back with that innocent gesture Annabel found almost unbearably sexy. "I was going for a walk and I thought I'd drop in."

"I'm glad," said Annabel. "Can I offer you a drink?" Even as she spoke, she was mortified. A drink! If Cody were dying of thirst she'd probably turn down a glass of water from her.

"Better not," Cody said. "Look where it got me last time." Her color heightened.

"I'm sorry . . ." both women began at the same time, then laughed awkwardly.

"Be my guest," Annabel offered with mock gallantry.

Cody started again. "I'm really sorry about the other night. I had too much to drink. I hope it wasn't too awful for you." She was backing down the verandah steps.

"Cody!" Annabel's tone arrested her. "Please don't go. I'm sorry too. You might find this hard to believe, but I don't make a habit of getting women drunk and having my wicked way with them."

Cody's mouth turned up into a smile. "You wouldn't have to try too hard, Annabel," she said wryly. "You're a very attractive woman."

"I find you very attractive too, Cody," Annabel said huskily. "The other night I . . ." She was embarrassed. "I guess I'm just sexually frustrated," she added in an attempt to laugh it off.

"How flattering," Cody responded with heavy irony.

Annabel raised one hand to her mouth. "Wonderful," she groaned. "Now I'm adding insult to injury." She stretched out a hand to Cody. "I'm sorry. Can we start again?"

Cody took the hand and allowed herself to be drawn up onto the verandah. They were looking straight into each other's eyes.

"I'd like to start again," Cody said very softly and the two women smiled at each other.

CHAPTER SIX

The days that followed passed in a blur for Annabel. She spent many hours poring over her aunt's diaries, trying to piece together the complex picture of her life. At times it was all she could do to concentrate. She found her thoughts straying constantly to Cody, wondering what she was doing, whether she was at home.

They saw each other every day, ate dinner together, walked along Passion Bay in the moonlight, occasionally brushed fingertips or thighs, but were not lovers.

Last night, on one of their strolls, Cody had slipped an arm around Annabel's waist and asked, "How did Passion Bay get its name?"

"I don't know," Annabel had replied. "I guess my aunt must have named it. She lived here for the past thirty years and this was her favorite beach. The Bay does have a certain reputation among the Islanders though."

"Oh yes," Cody prompted. "What's that?"

Annabel smiled. "Well, there's a legend. According to Mrs. Marsters, hundreds of years ago the Islanders believed that the waters of Passion Bay held the secret of fertility, so any woman who could not have a child would come here to bathe. A famous chief whose wife was barren — her fault, naturally — brought her to the island and left her here for three full cycles of the moon."

"Great way for her to get pregnant," Cody murmured.

"Indeed. Anyway, the story goes that he returned to pick her up and she had definitely conceived. In due course she gave birth to a daughter."

"So she was already pregnant when he left her here," Cody remarked. "I guess they didn't have test kits back then."

Annabel smiled. "No. Now this is where we get to the interesting bit. Evidently this woman was quite certain she actually conceived on the island. She claimed she was visited on a number of occasions by the goddess of the island, who lay with her and made her the gift of a child — the only one she had, as it turns out."

Cody's eyes widened. "Presumably this was after

the local missionary told all the heathen about the virgin birth?"

"Oh ye of little faith!" Annabel sighed. "No, it was way before then. And even more interesting is that no one lived on Moon Island except for a small group of women — the Island was sacred to women and men were forbidden. But the women who did live here had children, all girls."

"Very weird," said Cody. "So what do you make of all that?"

"Well there's really only one possible explanation."

"That the 'goddess' was a man in disguise?"

Annabel laughed. "Of course not!" She dug Cody lightly in the ribs. "It was parthenogenesis, the splitting of an egg without a sperm."

Cody looked dubious. "I thought scientists couldn't be sure about that."

"Do you really think they'd tell us if they could? Imagine that ... men not required for procreation."

Cody stopped in her tracks and grinned widely. "Women's eggs carry only an X chromosome ..."

"Now you're getting the picture. If parthenogenesis really can happen, it would result only in girls, and given we are the species type, that's not surprising."

"Oh dear," Cody commented. "The male-as-mutant argument. You're not a man-hating lesbian ball-breaker by any chance, are you?"

Annabel glanced at her sideways, sparkling. "Will I score any points if I say yes to that?"

"If you want to score points I have some more creative suggestions."

Annabel turned to face her, slid her arms behind

Cody's neck. "Nothing that could result in parthenogenesis, I hope."

She trailed slow sensual kisses down Cody's neck and onto her bare shoulders and they sank down onto the warm sands of Passion Bay. But as Annabel's fingers moved to the knot holding Cody's sarong, she felt the younger woman tense almost imperceptibly. Annabel pulled her close instead and rocked her gently, and they lay together listening to the sounds of the night.

Annabel knew with fatalistic certainty that they would become lovers, but her own feelings were mixed. She was wary of exposing herself. It was obvious that Cody was attracted to her, but she also sensed some confusion in the younger woman. That was hardly surprising. Cody had just been left by a long-term lover for a man. That would be enough to dent anyone's confidence.

Annabel could remember all too clearly those feelings of helpless rage, of self-blame and introspection when she broke up with Clare. For months afterward she had stared at herself in mirrors, wondering if there was something wrong with her, some defect only others could see. Even though the breakup had been more or less mutually agreed, she had still felt responsible. If only she were more political, Clare might have stayed, if only she looked more butch, if only she enjoyed demos as much as theater, if only she didn't sound like old money ... There was a list as long as her arm.

She had been so vulnerable then and so lonely. It was one of those times when she had most felt her isolation as a lesbian. When she'd broken up with Toby, after only six months of marriage, she had been inundated with support — phone calls from her mother, cuddles from friends and kindness from people at work. And she was the one who had left!

What a contrast with Clare. She'd been forced to pretend that everything was just fine and rosy in her world, that her housemate had got a new job in San Francisco and wasn't that great? Of course her lesbian friends understood and had comforted her. But for the first time in her life, Annabel had experienced deeply the distress of her invisibility. She had felt like two people, one the hard-working, successful banker, the other a secretive, distressed misfit.

Her parents were pleased, of course. Not because they wanted to see her hurt, but because they had always believed her sexuality could only lead to unhappiness. They perceived her break-up with Clare as a sign of their daughter coming to her senses. Her mother even referred to the possibility of another marriage now that she'd "got all that out of her system." Annabel didn't even bother to argue. What was the point?

Since that time she had barely mentioned the subject of her relationships to her parents and they never raised it. They knew she was still a lesbian, but it was not discussed and silences were nothing new in Annabel's family. For as long as she could remember, she had sensed the unspoken; the underground messages, her parents exchanging subtle glances, anger simmering beneath the quiet earth like a volcano. As a child, she had sometimes felt so nervous she had been unable to keep hold of her cutlery. And she had never understood why.

Dusting off another diary, Annabel shook her

head. The old trepidation was still there, that strange waiting feeling. Waiting for what? With curious unease she opened the book and began to read. It was 1959.

> *Rebecca has been wonderful. She won't let me feel ashamed for a moment. She's even bought me an island of all things, the goose. Mad isn't it? I have no idea how we are ever to get there but Rebecca says her family isn't in the shipping business for nothing and we leave as soon as the baby is born. I want to go now but Rebecca insists we must be near the hospital and as always she is the sensible one.*

A baby? Whose baby? Annabel's heart was thumping wildly and she hastily flicked back through the pages. Then she cursed and glanced at her watch. It was mercy mission time and Bevan Mitchell didn't appreciate his passengers not turning up.

With a sigh of impatience, Annabel closed the diary and climbed down the attic steps into her hallway. A baby? She gathered up her gear, donned her riding hat and stalked out, churning her discovery over in her mind.

Someone her Aunt knew, some close friend perhaps, had been having a baby. Or was it Rebecca? Aunt Annie was childless. Annabel knew that much. Again she felt that uneasy curling in the pit of her stomach and a nebulous image floated across her mind — herself as a tiny child, on a woman's knee, handling a large golden object and biting it. The woman's face was out of focus, but her hair was pale. *Mother,* Annabel thought. But she felt oddly disturbed.

CHAPTER SEVEN

"Cody! Cody!" Annabel reined Kahlo in close to Hibiscus Villa, tethered the horse and jumped the steps up to the open door. "Are you there, Cody? I've got something for you.

Cody emerged from the bathroom wearing a towel, her black hair wet and plastered to her head like a seal. Annabel pulled a sharp breath and let her eyes travel over the woman in front of her, enjoying the way the water rolled across Cody's smooth shoulders and followed the contours of her body to gather in rivulets between her breasts.

She held out a large paper bag and Cody took it with a questioning look. "Your mail," Annabel explained, and was puzzled as Cody's expression underwent a subtle change.

"Thanks," she said unenthusiastically and dropped the bag onto a small table nearby.

Annabel stayed where she was, flexing her whip slightly against one thigh and trying to pretend her muscles weren't taut with tension. "I'd love a cup of tea," she hinted finally.

"I'll get dressed," Cody said and turned back toward the bathroom.

"Look, am I interrupting something?"

Cody halted. "You know, Annabel," she said dully, "life can get very complicated."

Annabel pulled off her riding hat and flopped down into a cane chair. "Indeed it can," she agreed, staring at Cody's long, well muscled legs, her gaze halting where the towel began high on those damp thighs. Her mouth felt dry and her shirt too tight at the neck. Annabel eased a couple of buttons undone and tilted her head back, exposing her throat to the cool air drifting through the verandah.

Cody moved further into the house. "I'll put the tea on."

"No, I'll make it," Annabel offered quickly. "While you dress."

As she was stacking their cups onto the tray for the second time, having dropped everything on the floor in her first attempt, Cody appeared. She had changed into baggy white shorts and a thin lavender T-shirt and Annabel had the impression she had been crying.

"Are you all right, Cody?" She realized with a slight shock how much she actually cared.

Cody made a convincing display of unconcern, shrugging her shoulders and lifting the tray with a flourish. "I'm fine," she managed without a tremor. But she still looked everywhere but at Annabel.

They sat in silence performing the tea ritual. It was not a silence like the communion of old friends, or new friends completely at ease with one another. It was dense and clammy, and exaggerated by the piercing birdcalls and persistent drone of insects. It stretched like quicksand, deceptive, treacherous — neither woman willing to take an experimental step lest she sink out of her depth, uncertain of rescue.

Cody wanted to speak, but her throat was tight and her eyes still stung. Annabel looked so cool and somehow certain of the world. She would be shocked if Cody told her, shocked and probably disgusted to find she was calmly sipping tea with a criminal. Cody knew the secret put a barrier between them and she struggled to find the words to change that.

"Annabel," she finally plunged in. "Have you ever done something you regretted?"

Annabel's eyes widened. In the shade of the verandah they looked pansy-blue. She tilted her head to one side as though lost in thought, then said softly, "Something I've regretted? Gosh that gives me plenty of scope. I guess you don't mean taking a bath on the Yen either ..." She frowned and then admitted, "It's strange you should ask that. A few months ago I would have said no and wondered

70

what you were on about. But since I came to the
island, it's as if I've seen my life from a whole new
perspective. I've realized how miserable and empty it
was in Boston. I guess I was just so busy and so
tired back then, that I didn't have time to think
about what was missing."

She paused, picked up the question in Cody's
eyes and shook her head. "No, I didn't have time for
relationships either. I've had one or two flings." *Or
ten or twenty,* she thought cynically. "But nothing
serious. Maybe I've been horse shy." She said it
reflectively as though the idea were new and
interesting. "So to answer your question before you
fall asleep ... yes, I have done something I regret.
I'm feeling very sorry about the way I've spent my
life in the past four years. How about you?"

Cody sipped her tea and shifted in her seat, her
grey eyes intent. Annabel looked calm, reflective, a
little sad. Catching Cody's glance, she threw her a
reassuring smile and Cody fought off an
overwhelming urge to unburden herself completely.

How could she tell Annabel everything? They
barely knew each other and it was hardly fair to
involve another woman in her guilty secret. Yet it
would be such a relief to discuss it. Hardly an hour
passed that she didn't experience a sinking in her
stomach when she thought about that briefcase
lurking in Janet's wardrobe, or of a letter somewhere
recording her crime and demanding restitution.

She sighed and put her cup down with a clatter.
"I'm not sure that I have regrets, exactly," she said
honestly. "But I have done something that's making
me feel very guilty."

Annabel said nothing at first, but looked across

her cup at Cody with eyes that were curious, but also kind. "Sounds serious," she commented with a hint of humor and Cody relaxed despite herself.

"It is. I can't talk about it right now but it's on my mind a lot and I guess I wanted you to know so you wouldn't think I'm unfriendly or rude."

"Is it important what I think?" Annabel asked quietly. She leaned forward, cupping her chin in one hand and examining Cody's face with unnerving intensity.

Cody blushed and lowered her eyes. It *was* important, but she found herself wishing it weren't. Since last night on the beach, she'd hardly been able to get Annabel out of her mind. Even now her skin tingled at the memory of Annabel's mouth, her warmth.

Don't! she ordered herself. The very last thing she needed in her life right now was another complication. Forcing a lighter note, she said casually, "Of course it is. You're supposed to be wildly impressed with my good looks, charm and incisive wit. Back home, the girls can't leave me alone."

Annabel rolled her eyes, clutched her chest and simpered, "I can sure see why that is. The first time I laid eyes on you, well, I just said to myself, Annabel honey, this is your lucky day ..."

Cody grinned at the Southern Belle impersonation. "You betcha." She affected a pose that drew attention to her neatly muscled arms. "They don't call me hotlips for nothing."

Annabel groaned. "Hotlips, how original." She studied Cody's mouth blatantly. "I take it you have a reputation?"

Cody nodded. "Yeah. Ever since a bad moment with a chili taco at the Refuge fundraiser, in fact."

Annabel laughed. "Cramped your style?"

"For weeks." Cody grinned then puckered her lips. "I thought I'd never be the same woman again."

"And are you?" Annabel's gaze traveled warmly across her body.

Not yet, Cody's mind ordered, but her body was not convinced. Her pulse had quickened and she found herself unable to look away from Annabel's face — the way the fine stray hairs escaped from her plait and curled damply on her forehead, the way her lips turned up slightly in the corners and her chin dimpled when she laughed.

When Annabel got to her feet, Cody felt a sharp pang of disappointment.

"I should be going," she was saying without conviction. She scanned Cody's face, a hint of challenge in those bright lavender eyes, then glanced about as though looking for something.

"My whip," she explained and moved past Cody to reach for it. Then her hands were on Cody's shoulders and Cody could feel the warmth of her as she leaned over the chair back. Her skin burned where Annabel was touching it. She twisted in her chair to look up at the other woman.

"Annabel ..." she began awkwardly, then chickened out. "Um, have a nice day," she said, trying to sound normal.

To Cody's consternation, Annabel bent lower, letting her arms slide from Cody's shoulders past her breasts, and she rested her head lightly against Cody's.

"Why don't you come, too," she invited softly. Her

warm breath brushed Cody's cheek. Cody inhaled that familiar Annabel fragrance and swallowed with difficulty.

"You might even enjoy it," Annabel persisted. She moved around the chair to face Cody, and with a broad smile took both her hands and pulled her to her feet.

She was very close and this time Cody let herself stare. At point blank Annabel's skin was the radiant creamy white of a fine pearl. Cody found herself fascinated by its texture, by the natural red of Annabel's mouth against it, the denseness of her lashes. She imagined brushing it with her fingers, her lips, her tongue, and she felt a flowering in her groin.

Annabel was watching her with a frank expression, a hint of humor in the back of those amethyst eyes, and Cody realized she must be gawking like some star struck adolescent. She lowered her gaze quickly and pulled her hands free. Her heart was pounding against her ribs like a trapped bird and she felt altogether too exposed.

"I won't come, thanks." She had finally gathered her wits enough to speak but her voice sounded hoarse, unlike her own. She took a step back, wanting to distance herself from Annabel, from the chaotic emotions the other woman was arousing. Her skin was tingling, aching for touch.

Annabel bent, picked up her whip and flexed it absently. Cody was looking to one side, hands tucked defensively into her armpits. Annabel felt a powerful urge to reach for her. She studied the outline of Cody's breasts flattened beneath her folded arms and imagined pulling those hands away, touching her nipples beneath. She felt guilty then; conscious of her own sexual arousal, and of Cody's obvious discomfort.

Cody had only just broken up with her lover and hadn't had time to heal, Annabel reminded herself. It would be all too easy, she thought, disgusted with herself. Seducing a woman on the rebound — now that was a class act, the kind she'd become famous for after her break-up with Clare.

Back then, she had adopted a love 'em and leave 'em approach to relationships and had spent a year proving she could fuck any woman she liked, whenever she liked, and feel nothing. To whom she was proving it was a moot point. When she finally made the switch into stock trading, she had been secretly relieved. The long hours and exhausting routine had soon provided the excuse she needed to slide out of any kind of commitment, and before long hanging over a screen and shouting into a phone in each hand gave her a bigger rush than an orgasm.

At the time she had been delighted — cheap thrills without the emotional hassles of relationships. Now she felt sick at the thought of the women she must have hurt along the way.

Thank God she was past all that now. It really was different with Cody. Certainly she recognized the powerful sexual vibes between them, but there was something else too. A tenderness, an urge to find out more about Cody. Feelings she would have run a mile from only months ago.

Impulsively Annabel took a couple of paces toward Cody and lifted one hand to her face, cradling it and tilting it to meet hers. She ran a gentle thumb across Cody's bottom lip and felt her mouth part slightly, automatically. Then she brushed the parted lips with her own very softly and felt Cody's body sway into hers, felt the warmth of her thighs, the brush of her nipples.

"I could stay," she murmured, delicately sampling Cody's mouth and sliding her hand beneath her T-shirt to bring her closer.

Cody dropped her protective arms, moving them slowly around Annabel. "I'd like that."

They looked at each other intently. Everything seemed very still in the sultry languor of the afternoon. Annabel was conscious only of Cody; her soft shallow breathing, the wanting in her eyes.

But something was tugging at her. She gave a slight, bemused start, looked around and groaned. "Oh, no."

A pair of dark liquid eyes surveyed her inquisitively, and Kahlo prised the whip she was still holding from her fingers.

Cody looked startled. "I thought she was tied up."

"I'm sorry." Annabel shook her head, disbelieving. "I'll put her in the lean-to around the back." She touched Cody's face. "Don't go away."

It was a tragic piece of timing, Cody decided as she went into the villa. In more ways than one. It would have been so easy to fall into bed with Annabel right then and there. But reality had intervened and pulled her up short.

It was probably for the best, Cody convinced herself. Not only was she fresh out of a broken relationship, but she was also a fugitive from justice.

She raked despondent fingers through her hair and paced the sitting room. Her mind seethed with conflicting emotions. She wanted to make love with Annabel — her body was unmistakably clear about that. But her life was a mess. *She* was a mess; a walking rebound disaster. How could she even contemplate getting involved with another woman?

Lamenting her folly, she crept onto the sofa and buried her face in a cushion. A moment later someone touched her shoulder.

"Have you changed your mind?" Annabel sat down beside her.

Embarrassed, Cody straightened up. "No ... I mean ..."

"It's okay." Annabel reached out and pushed the hair back from her forehead. "I understand."

"No." Cody caught at her hand. She felt trapped, beached on the disorienting sands of her own insecurity. "Please. Don't go."

Annabel held her, stroked her head gently. "We don't have to *do* anything, you know." There was a hint of amusement in her voice. "I'd like to, of course." She tilted Cody's chin and stared at her intently. Then she bent forward and kissed her.

They sat very still, mouths just touching. Cody closed her eyes. Annabel's breath was warm on her face. She moved against her, placing her hands behind her neck and responding to her kisses.

By some unspoken consensus, they moved to Cody's bedroom and stood there kissing until Cody felt hot and weak. Annabel's mouth moved to her face and throat, her hands unfastening Cody's shorts. Panic fluttered along with desire in the pit of Cody's stomach and her breath came in short, shallow gasps. She turned her attention to Annabel's shirt, unbuttoning it and sliding it off her shoulders.

Annabel's skin glowed with all the richness of ivory silk and begged to be touched. Cody stared, wanting at the same time to taste it, smell it.

"You're beautiful," she whispered and lowered her head to plant devotional kisses along Annabel's shoulders, slowly working her way down to her small breasts and those nipples, the same astounding dark pink as her mouth.

She pulled off her T-shirt, longing to press her flesh against Annabel's, to remove the final layers between them. Annabel was unzipping her jeans and Cody helped tug them over her hips, impatience making her a little rough.

With a soft laugh, Annabel stepped out of them and reached for Cody's hands, raising them to her mouth and kissing them tenderly. "Not so fast," she said, and moved her lips to Cody's, kissing her lightly, teasingly.

Cody drew a ragged breath, caught hold of Annabel's hips and pulled her determinedly toward the bed.

"Why not fast?" she said, throwing back the covers and drawing Annabel down with her. She felt sick with passion, wanted Annabel inside her, around her, close and hot.

Annabel's hands were on her shoulders, pressing them down, as she knelt across Cody's body, astride one thigh so Cody could feel her wetness. She bent to kiss Cody's face, just brushing the skin with her lips until Cody's mouth parted, trembling and full, and she whispered Annabel's name, then gasped as fingers found her clitoris, slid down to sample her wetness then moved casually back again.

Cody lifted her hips, wanting more than the slow teasing strokes. She opened heavy eyes and met Annabel's, dark, intense purple, the pupils dilated. She reached up, slid her fingers into Annabel's hair and pulled her down to kiss her passionately, reveling in the foreign textures of her body. Her breasts felt firm, the nipples hard. She was hot and smooth, as supple as a cat.

Annabel slipped her hands beneath Cody's shoulders and pulled her upright so they were both on their knees and each was free to explore the newness of the other's body. Cody pressed hard, loving the way their stomachs, their mounds, connected. She stretched exploring fingers out across Annabel's buttocks, kneading the firm flesh, and drew her hips further forward, sighing with pleasure as the pressure on her clitoris increased.

Annabel's fingers were working their own magic, stroking and caressing Cody's breasts, rolling her nipples into tense arousal. They were followed by her mouth and Cody's skin shocked and tightened at the small, soft bites.

"Don't stop," she murmured as Annabel moved further down her body, tracing small circles around her stomach and down into the mound of hair. Determined fingers parted her thighs and Cody swayed, then clutched Annabel's shoulders as she felt the head of her clitoris enveloped slowly, wetly.

She felt hot, breathless. Tiny beads of

perspiration clustered on her forehead and she released small soft cries of pleasure. "Don't stop," she begged again, as Annabel pulled back.

The other woman straightened, her fingers taking up where her tongue left off. She aligned her body with Cody's, staring into her eyes with frank desire. Then she placed one hand firmly behind Cody's head and kissed her hard, entering her at the same time with insistent fingers.

"You feel good inside," she said against Cody's mouth and Cody could taste herself. She wanted to touch Annabel too, make her cry out with pleasure, but instead she grasped her, steadying herself as her limbs shook and her arousal climbed unbearably.

Annabel held her close, lowered her to the bed, slid a hand under her buttocks, tilting her up to move deeper inside. Cody was shaking and sweating, her body open, craving. Annabel's tongue was circling her clitoris again and Cody moved her hips to meet the voluptuous rhythm.

She wanted to speak, but could only gasp. She bit her lip as the tension in her body climbed to breaking point, then snapped in a hot, pulsing swell of pleasure. It rushed through her, forcing a hoarse cry from her lips and a final startling burst of moisture from every pore.

Then Annabel was kissing her face tenderly and Cody realized she was crying. She stared up at Annabel, suddenly self-conscious.

Annabel smiled warmly. "You're fine, Cody," she said as she pushed the damp hair off Cody's forehead to plant a kiss there.

When Cody stretched out exploring fingers her

hand was caught gently and she was pulled into Annabel's arms.

"Later," Annabel murmured between kisses. "I'm not going anywhere just at the moment."

And as the hours passed and a full moon swam placidly across Passion Bay, they made love again and again until exhaustion overtook them and, curling into each other, they slept.

It was dawn when Cody awoke. She lay very still watching the sky transform and listening to the birds and insects come alive. Annabel was still sleeping, her thick lashes resting on her cheeks like two dark crescents. Her hair, released from its tight plait the night before, lay tangled about her head, and her mouth was curved delectably upward as though she were dreaming clouds of butterflies.

Cody looked at her in near disbelief. She had just spent the past night making love with this woman, exploring every inch of her body, finding the secret places that made her writhe and beg for more. She was beautiful, stunning. Cody grinned broadly and snuggled closer to the sleeping Annabel.

She had no idea where this would lead, and for the moment it didn't seem to matter. Her body felt warm, used, content. Her mind was clear and fresh. Best of all, she could think of Margaret and ... nothing. No tears, no rage, nothing. You shallow person, a voice chastised her. Only six weeks to mend a broken heart. The first attractive woman that comes along and wham! Margaret's history.

Cody lifted a strand of Annabel's hair. It was fine and silky, nearly white. The kind of hair chemicals couldn't reproduce. Cody wished Annabel would wear it loose all the time, but guessed she was far too practical for that.

In the two weeks since she had met Annabel, every one of her unconscious assumptions had been turned inside out. Somehow she had never imagined herself with a blonde American lover who looked like she thought hard work was a day's shopping in Saks, but fixed her own plumbing without batting an eyelid.

Annabel was a mass of contradictions. Sometimes she seemed entirely cynical and world-weary. Then she would rush outside to catch the first evening star or stand stock-still on her lawn trying to persuade a mynah bird to eat from her outstretched hand.

During the time they had explored the island together Cody had been astounded at Annabel's knowledge of plants and birdlife, her navigation skills and her fitness. She *was* once a Girl Scout, Annabel had said.

Cody slipped an arm over her body and kissed her forehead gently. Two weeks. A thought strayed across her mind. Her Moon Island booking ran out in two week's time. What then? London? Some tiny flat in Highgate ... wall-to-wall commuters ... cliquey parties. Maybe she should head for Australia instead. Melbourne was a laid-back kind of city, plenty of jobs.

Cody frowned. She didn't want to think about leaving, especially now. But how could she stay? Even if she booked another month on the island, that would only be a short-term solution. If anything it would make leaving that much harder. Besides she had no idea what Annabel's plans were — when she intended to return to Boston. Cody's heart lurched and almost unconsciously she tightened her arms.

Annabel stirred, opening her eyes dazedly, then smiling when she met Cody's gaze. "Hi," she said, sliding her arms around Cody. "Do you still respect me?"

Cody grinned. "Well that depends," she said playfully.

Annabel lifted her eyebrows. "Oh really? Depends on what?"

"On whether you can rustle up a decent breakfast, of course." Cody changed position, lounging back on her pillows, hands behind her head.

"Why how very butch of you, Cody Stanton." Annabel's eyes gleamed. "Do I detect a hint of role confusion here?" She propped herself up onto her elbow and trailed a knowing hand down Cody's body, applying just enough teasing pressure to Cody's clitoris to make her squirm deliciously.

"Now don't get all excited," she whispered against Cody's ear, then nibbled her lobe. "After all, I'm about to go get intimate with your kitchen." She drew back, slid her feet off the bed and stretched languorously.

"Oh no you don't," Cody crawled after her, giggling. "I take it all back."

"Too late." Annabel located a sarong and began to wrap it around herself. "I wouldn't want you lying in bed suffering from *cravings*." She slapped Cody's hands as Cody tried to untie her sarong.

"What do you feel like eating?" Her tone was business-like, but her eyes sparkled. "Something hot?"

"Precisely," said Cody and grabbed her around the waist. "Come back to bed, you flirt."

"Make it worth my while," said Annabel.

And Cody did.

🙿 🙿 🙿 🙿 🙿

"I have to go." Annabel slid her arms around Cody's waist and kissed the corner of her mouth. "I hear the whine of a lone Dominie somewhere in the blur beyond."

Cody grimaced and followed Annabel outside in time to see the Dominie slouch its way across the sky.

"Can't he go without you for once?" she muttered.

Annabel was saddling Kahlo and pushing her shirt into her loose-fitting jeans. She shook her head. "Duty calls, I'm afraid. If I don't go to Rarotonga we don't eat."

Annabel wished she could stay. Cody was looking so dejected standing in the doorway, her unbrushed hair sticking out at crazy angles, grey eyes wide and appealing. Annabel felt curiously protective and she was startled at the emotion and not entirely comfortable with it. Feeling protective smacked of ownership, of lack of boundaries. In her experience it was a trap for the unwary. It meant losing touch with your common sense and sometimes your self-respect. The last time she had felt protective, she'd sold herself short, allowed a woman to manipulate her, and been hurt. She knew better than to do that again.

With a hint of reserve in her eyes, she looked back at Cody and willed herself not to respond to the unspoken plea. "Come over to my place for dinner," she said and mounted Kahlo with easy grace.

"Okay," Cody said quietly.

Annabel tried not to notice the slight hurt in her voice. She could feel Cody watching her as she reined the mare away from the villa, but she did not look back.

Bevan was waiting when she reached the landing strip and he greeted her past his habitual cigarette.

Annabel boarded without ceremony and strapped herself in. She was fast coming to take for granted the two-hour shuttle to and from the island. They went to Rarotonga every second day and brought in fresh supplies, taxied guests and Mrs. Marsters, the housekeeper, and collected mail.

At first the battered plane had unnerved Annabel, and Bevan's comment that he could fly her under the Golden Gate if necessary, had done little to inspire confidence. Annabel hated the helpless, dependent feeling of being an ignorant passenger, of staring at the flickering needles on the control panel without the slightest idea what any of them meant.

To her surprise, Bevan had been quick to notice her attitude and had promptly offered to teach her to fly. He had pointed out that the Dominie was originally used as a navigation trainer for the English RAF. The plane was built during World War II, originally for six passengers, but after the war it had found its way into private ownership in Australia and eventually Bevan had swapped a bag of opals for it at Broken Hill.

He had converted it to a two-passenger and cargo transport, and had flown charter through most of Southeast Asia and the Pacific. Annabel's Aunt had employed him six years ago when he settled on Atiu, the island whose coffee was the best Annabel had ever tasted. He still lived there with a friend she had never met, but who was evidently some kind of journalist.

Annabel had been amazed at how easy it was to learn to fly, and with every lesson she became more confident.

"Feel like taking her up today?" Bevan asked, securing the hatch.

She smiled wryly. "I don't think I'm quite ready for that." She'd tried last time and they had bunny-hopped the entire length of the strip twice before Bevan took the controls back and got them off the ground.

"They're like horses, Annabel," the pilot told her. "You just have to keep climbing back in the saddle."

"Okay," she said resignedly. "It's your funeral. But just don't ask me to land the thing."

Bevan only wiggled his cigarette, the equivalent of a grin, then made a show of stubbing it out, ready to do business. "Full throttle," he ordered blithely.

Annabel had no idea how they managed to get to Rarotonga. By some fluke she had coerced the

Dominie into the air and as they approached the island, Bevan radioed for clearance. Then he cheerfully informed Annabel that he would talk her down.

"Land her? I can't!" Annabel protested.

"Most popular words in the female dialect," he goaded her. Then he informed her that landing was no big deal and since they were nearly out of fuel she'd better quit mucking around.

"Oh great!" Annabel glared at the gauge and turned accusing eyes on Bevan. "You're paid to make sure that doesn't happen!"

"Watch your back pressure," she was told.

"Bevan!" Her hands began to shake.

"Keep your nose up," he said blandly.

He continued firing instructions at her, so there was no time to do anything but obey. Putting her anger aside, Annabel concentrated on her landing transition. They came in with a resounding thud and veered waywardly along the strip while she tried to sort out her rudder control. When they finally stopped, back-to-front and off the runway, Annabel let out a whoop and collapsed forward with relief and exhilaration.

"Well done, old girl." Bevan shook her hand with British formality and Annabel felt her anger dissolve.

"I really did it," she marveled as they taxied back across the tarmac. "I flew a plane!"

They jumped down onto the hot tarmac and Bevan lit a cigarette and blew a small smoke ring. "Yep. Last time I talked a novice down was in 'Nam."

"You fought in Vietnam?" Annabel eyed him suspiciously.

"No," he replied. "I ran supplies. A spot of black market here and there."

"Racketeering," she said grimly.

"Beats slaughter any day. You sleep a whole lot better too."

Annabel said nothing.

"Oh, by the way ..." Bevan fished about in his pockets. "I picked this up for you." He handed her a folded notice. "Compliments of the local constabulary."

Annabel raised questioning eyes, opened the sheet out and stared, knuckles whitening.

"But it's ..."

Bevan sucked on his cigarette. "Thought I recognized one of your guests."

Annabel examined the photograph and the caption underneath. *Cordelia Grace Stanton.*

"The police ..." she murmured.

"Seems they're concerned for her safety," Bevan observed.

Annabel's brow creased. "Have you ..."

He shook his head and she slid the poster into her bag.

"I'll take care of it," she told him with more confidence than she felt.

Back on the island later that afternoon, Annabel paced agitatedly about her house. Her brains felt scrambled, her nerves on edge. One part of her wanted to rush straight over to Cody and ask her what was going on, another told her to mind her own business.

The poster said information was wanted by her family. Perhaps they were incredibly possessive of her, Annabel reasoned. Perhaps she'd had to disappear just to get some privacy. Some families were like that. But nonetheless, Cody didn't seem the type of woman who would vanish without a word, leaving people worried for her safety. And if she had, surely it would be a good idea to get in touch with them so they could give up bothering the police and pasting up wanted posters.

Annabel made herself a double espresso and examined the poster for about the thousandth time. What was it Cody had said the day before about something she regretted, something that made her feel guilty? This must be it, Annabel decided. She's lost her lover and her job and she needed some space. Without really thinking it through, she had picked an island in the middle of nowhere and gone. Her family, knowing she was upset, had panicked ... Or, on second thought, maybe her family knew nothing about her lesbianism and therefore wouldn't understand what she was going through. It was probably asking a bit much for anyone to come out to her parents at the same time as her lover had walked out on her.

Annabel sipped her coffee and chewed her bottom lip. She wished Cody would open up to her a bit more. All she really knew about her family was that her parents had separated when she was much younger. She had no idea whether Cody got on with her mother, whether she had sisters or brothers, or anyone else close to her in Wellington. With a sudden pang, she wondered whether they needed to get in touch with her because of some emergency.

Someone might be sick, or worse. Annabel's thoughts strayed to her aunt and she frowned again.

It was all very peculiar, she decided. But Cody would be around soon and no doubt she would have a simple explanation for everything.

⁊⁊ ⁊ ⁊ ⁊ ⁊

With reluctant fingers, Cody tore open her mail and stacked her letters in an orderly pile. There were several from Janet herself, plus a large bundle she had tied together to forward on. The long white envelope with the embossed logo stuck out like a sore thumb and Cody decided to read the bad news first.

The letter was polite and to the point. It told her how much her employers regretted the need to downsize and how they wished her all the best in her next career move. She was not to hesitate if they could assist her in any way with a new employer and to that end a reference was enclosed.

Disbelief mounting, Cody read the said reference and told herself to breathe. It was full of glowing comments about her skills, reliability and self-motivation. It promised any prospective employers that they would be getting a good deal and it said nothing whatsoever about ninety thousand missing dollars.

They didn't know, Cody realized with a shock. It was almost anticlimactic. Here she was convincing herself that she would have to leave the islands — probably in the dead of night in a cargo boat —

90

change identity, dye her hair, get a tattoo. But no. Those incompetents in the accounting division hadn't even noticed yet. How typical!

Cody leaned heavily into the soft couch and sighed. She felt almost drunk with relief. She could stay! Maybe they'd just write it off as some mysterious accounting glitch and it would be swallowed, like most things inexplicable, in the mists of time.

"Never," she muttered to herself. Come the audit, they would leap on that extra zero like a shoal of piranhas and that would be the end of Cody Stanton's life of crime. She shuddered, wondering how long she had.

Janet's letters were mostly gossip and complaints about the weather. Cody was reaching the end of them when a name leapt out at her. Margaret. She had rung, Janet said, and asked for Cody's address. *She wants to see you,* Janet had written in her scrawling purple ink. *She says there's something she needs to talk about.* According to Janet she seemed upset, especially because Cody had gone without discussing her plans.

Cody snorted. Since when did you ring up your ex-lover who's just traded you in for beefcake and say, By the way, dear, I'm so traumatized about the way you've treated me that I'm leaving for a month's peace and quiet on a tropical island. Here's the address.

What a nerve! And to cap it off, Scott, her bloke, also had his boxers in a twist. *Margaret says Scott is very worried, he cares about you too.* Janet had added a few exclamation marks of her own. Cody felt like ripping that page up and ritually burning it. Scott cares too ... How touching, how very liberal of him. What a guy.

"Jerk," she said, and wondered all over again how a woman of Margaret's intelligence could have been taken in by a BMW and a bunch of smarmy platitudes. Scott Drysdale was about as plausible as the Animal Liberation Front browsing a fur shop.

What did Margaret want? Their coffee machine, or maybe half the bed linen? Perhaps she'd discovered her Ferron tape missing. Cody glanced across at her ghetto blaster with a smug expression. Petty, a little voice prodded, very petty. But Cody ignored it and continued reading her mail.

There was no other long white envelope, no court summons, no solicitor's letter. Nothing. Cody wished the queasy feeling in her stomach would leave. It was ridiculous. She had some breathing space. They hadn't found out yet, but she found herself almost wishing they had. At least then she wouldn't be faced with another week of uncertainty, of waiting for the ax to fall.

Cody resented it. None of this trivia should be able to interfere with her holiday, but it did. Here she was, preparing to go round to a new lover's house for the evening, probably the night, and all she could think about was a briefcase full of banknotes in her best friend's bedroom.

Poor Janet. What if she found out? What if she was somehow caught with the goods? That would make her an accessory. Cody cringed. Theirs was an indestructible friendship, and Janet would love her no matter what — but arrested? That could be pushing her luck.

Cody cleared the pile of letters away and went inside. Looking around her bedroom, she couldn't help but smile rather foolishly. The bed was a shameless mess, mattress askew, sheets untucked and duvet languishing on the floor.

A wrist watch and some small pearl studs sat on the window ledge and Cody examined them with careful fingers. She sighed, felt a telltale wetness between her legs and poked her head out the window to search the sky. She wanted to go round to Villa Luna now. She wanted to hold Annabel, bury herself in her. The strength of her feelings came as almost a physical blow. It's a holiday romance, she tried to tell herself, a brief intense encounter; safe because it offers no future.

She had never had a "fling," although there'd been no shortage of offers. Her only other lover apart from Margaret had been her first: May, thoughtful, introspective and academic. They had met as students, both in Women's Studies. May had offered to help Cody with an essay and then calmly seduced her. Their relationship had lasted nearly two years until May returned with her parents to Canada. By that time they were more like deep friends than lovers and Cody was not even entirely sure how the transition had occurred.

She had never fully understood the dynamics of that relationship. She'd had nothing to measure it against. May had never asked for monogamy but Cody hadn't imagined anything else. At first she had been shocked to find May had other lovers and she was also puzzled at her choices — always a new lesbian.

"It's my duty," May had told her very seriously. "Women coming out need careful handling, a happy introduction to lesbianism. It's the least I can offer."

It sounded hilarious but May had been deadly serious, Cody realized. And in retrospect, she too was grateful for that careful handling.

May had a child now, a three-year-old daughter. She lived with her lover in Montreal. *Come and see us*, she had written to Cody earlier in the year. Cody thought about that invitation. She gathered up her bikini and headed off to Passion Bay. She had just enough time for a swim before she went to Annabel's.

"So here you are!"

Cody rolled over and squinted into the fading sun. "How was Avarua?" she asked.

"Hot." Annabel lowered herself to the sand next to Cody. She wore her dark glasses and big shady hat, and Cody couldn't see enough of her face to tell what she was thinking but her voice seemed strained. All that flying backward and forward, Cody thought. It was no wonder.

"Why do you have to go over all the time?" she demanded, "Is it some kind of job?"

"You could say that," Annabel nodded. "It sort of came with the house."

"You're in charge of the island?"

Annabel's mouth tightened slightly. "Cody," she

protested. "Why the third degree? What is it you want to know exactly?"

Cody shrugged, backed off a little. "I guess I just wanted to know why you're stuck with flying into Rarotonga with some man all the time. I'm jealous already."

Annabel laughed throatily. "You're most welcome to come if you want to. We could do with the extra ballast."

Cody cringed dramatically. "Forget it," she said. "I'll only be flying in that antique when I absolutely have to."

"Oh, it's not so bad," Annabel defended. She was about to add that she had been flying the Dominie herself but thought the better of it. She could imagine Cody worrying herself sick with lurid fantasies about air crashes. She stretched out a hand and caressed Cody's stomach, hooking her thumb into the narrow bikini briefs.

"Nude sunbathing is allowed here, you know."

"You don't say." Cody lifted her hips slightly to enable the briefs to be discarded. Her top soon followed and Annabel stretched out alongside her, sliding her hands the length of Cody's body.

"You're delicious," she murmured, then felt an unwelcome pang of guilt. She had come down to the beach to show Cody the poster and ask her what was going on, not to make love to her. But she was loath to spoil the mood.

The air was very warm and with the fading sun a mild breeze rustled the palms. The shadows were deepening around them. Soon the sky would flush pink and the first stars would appear. Annabel didn't want to let those precious hours slip away talking about something she already knew made Cody feel uncomfortable. They had so little time as it was.

The thought jolted her like a bucket of cold water. So little time ...

"Cody," she paused in between kissing her shoulders. "When do you go back home?"

Cody's grey eyes took a moment to focus. "Home?" She sat up, gathered her towel about her and examined Annabel's face with a guarded expression. "I leave the island in fifteen days." Her voice was dull and Annabel groaned inwardly. So much for not spoiling the mood.

She slid an arm around Cody's shoulders. "Sorry, that was about as romantic as a tuna sandwich before bed."

"It's okay," Cody said. "I've been thinking about it too." She tried to sound blasé. "You know the kind of thing. Will we ever see each other again or are these just a couple of weeks we won't be telling our grandchildren about in years to come."

She got to her feet, tied the towel around her waist and shook the sand out of her hair. Her skin had already tanned a rich caramel brown, except for her breasts which clearly showed the marks of her bikini.

She was upset. Annabel sensed it and felt her own confusion surface. "Cody." She scrambled to her feet and caught the other woman's arm. "I ... this is not just a holiday fling for me. I want you to know that."

Cody turned to face her and her eyes darkened

to raincloud grey. "Annabel," she began, then seemed to change her mind and shrugged half-heartedly. "Let's not make this complicated." The words sounded odd, stilted, "I mean, this is the grownups . . ."

"Cody!" Annabel broke in. "What are you saying? That you want nothing more than a meaningless affair?"

Cody lowered her gaze, screening the feelings she knew must show.

Her silence frustrated Annabel. "Cody, I'm not Margaret. I don't want to say goodbye to you in a week or so and never lay eyes on you again."

"Well what *do* you want then?" Cody demanded.

"I want to give whatever is happening between us a chance. Cody, please." She tightened her grip on Cody's arm. "Why are you being so defensive?"

Cody stared down at the fingers and shook her head slowly. "Oh, Annabel. It's just so complicated."

"Cody, you can trust me." Annabel drew closer, her arms sliding around Cody. She wanted Cody to speak to her, tell her whatever had to be told of her own volition. Annabel could sense an internal struggle in her, something hidden. It raised a wall between them, and if they were to have any chance at all, that would have to change. And Annabel knew suddenly that she wanted them to have a chance. She wanted it badly.

She was pushing Cody too hard, she realized, demanding a level of trust there hadn't been time to establish. And, not surprisingly, Cody was running in the opposite direction. That was what all the mixed messages were about.

Annabel loosened her arms and reached up to stroke Cody's hair gently. This was one woman she didn't want to frighten off. The poster could wait.

"Where did you grow up, Cody?" Annabel asked the woman in her arms later that night.

"On a farm," Cody responded drowsily, and nuzzled Annabel's breast. "In a place called Waipukurau. Until I was twelve."

"And then?"

"In Wellington city. The place with the permanent wind machine."

"Your family moved?"

"No. My mother did, when she separated from my father."

"Any sisters or brothers?"

"Just one brother," Cody said quietly. "He was killed in a car accident when I was sixteen."

Annabel felt her stiffen, caught the unmistakable edge of grief in her voice. Instinctively she tightened her embrace. "You were close?"

"Twins," Cody said. "When my parents separated Charles stayed with Dad and we only saw each other on holidays. It was awful. Up till then we had done everything together. We had a lot of fun." She smiled, memories flooding. "One thing we used to do all the time was dress up in each other's clothes and fool people, even our teachers. We looked so alike, you see."

"That must have been incredible," Annabel remarked, fascinated at the idea. "Did you notice any difference in how people treated you when you were dressed as a boy?"

"Hell yes!" Cody laughed. "One thing that really got me was putting up my hand in class. When I was Charles and put up my hand to answer a question or volunteer, I always got picked. Normally I could have chopped my arm off and thrown it at the teacher and she wouldn't have noticed me."

"Sounds typical," Annabel said. "What about at home?"

"We couldn't get away with it around Mom. She always knew. But it was a different story with Dad." She thought about her father, always distracted with something.

Back then, when Cody had asked her mother why she was leaving him, she had said it was because of her hair. She'd had it dyed blonde.

But what's wrong with that? a twelve-year-old Cody had demanded.

Your father doesn't like it.

So who cares what he thinks? Cody had stamped her foot. *Anyway it's been like that for months now.*

That's the whole point, Cordelia, her mother had said in her quiet way. *He only just noticed.*

Cody shook herself back to the present. "Dad was always too busy to notice us kids."

Annabel murmured sympathetically, then asked, "What was it like growing up in your country?"

Cody paused. "I've never given it much thought. New Zealand's a small place and Waipukurau, where I was raised, is what you might call a one-horse town. It's the kind of place the film crews hire to make retro ads and they don't have to change a thing." She snuggled closer and ran her hand over Annabel's warm curves. "It's a very beautiful country, Annabel, all green and natural. Tourists go wild about the place but I guess when you live there you take it for granted. We call it Godzone."

"And you're called Kiwis aren't you, like the fruit?"

"That's right. But in reality the Kiwi is a rather fat flightless bird that sleeps all day and comes out at night."

Annabel laughed softly. "Sounds like half of San Francisco," she quipped. "So what sort of things did you do as a kid?"

"God, that feels so long ago ... I went to school on a bus that stopped at the farm gate, then later I went to a girls' boarding school. My brother and I ran wild a bit, although it was all pretty harmless — like trying to blow up the neighbor's mailbox with fireworks on Guy Fawkes Day, and driving Dad's Land Rover into the river when we were ten."

"It sounds wonderful."

There was a wistful note in Annabel's voice and Cody looked up at her, but was unable to make out her expression in the moonlight. "What about you?" she asked. "Were you born in Boston?"

Annabel opened her mouth to say yes, but paused as that image repeated in her consciousness — herself on a woman's knee, playing with something shiny. "I've lived there ever since I can remember," she answered.

"Were you happy?" Cody asked.

Annabel felt her eyes sting suddenly. "I had everything a child could want," she said, thinking of her huge doll collection, her pony, her endless wardrobe of expensive dresses.

"Mmmm," Cody nodded sleepily. "But were you happy?"

"Happy?" Annabel felt her heart thump erratically. Of course she was happy. She had the perfect family, didn't she? The beautiful people, Clare had always called her parents. Annabel had the kind of life that was the envy of most children, certainly nothing to complain about. She had always scorned the poor-little-rich-girl syndrome. She was lucky and she knew it. But happy?

"No," she finally admitted in a whisper. "No I wasn't happy."

Cody did not reply, and listening to her deep even breathing, Annabel knew she was asleep. For a long time she just lay there, plagued with that image of the woman and the shiny thing, and with a lurking uneasiness in the back of her mind.

CHAPTER EIGHT

Cody dug her toes into the wet sand and gazed at the horizon. The beach was deserted and the sun too newly risen to have gathered strength. Wading along the water's edge, she was deep in thought. A week. She and Annabel had been lovers for a week and already Cody could not conceive of a future without her.

But what kind of future did they have? Since that uneasy conversation on the beach three days ago, they had avoided the whole topic, as if some unspoken agreement existed to live only for the moment. They spent most of their time together, and found that they had the oddest things in common. They both liked their eggs barely cooked and without salt, they had both broken their collarbones when they were eight, they both had stamp collections they couldn't bear to part with.

Cody was often conscious of Annabel's lavender eyes on her, a question in their depths — and something else. Sadness? She couldn't be sure. Cody felt confused, torn. When she was with Annabel she was gloriously happy, her flesh singing. When they made love she surrendered herself totally to the experience, feeling a powerful sense of belonging.

Sometimes she fancied irrationally that she had been waiting for Annabel all her life, that nothing mattered until now. In those moments she saw herself with startling clarity, marveled at the meaningless trivia of her life, hated herself for doubting the future, for all the fears that surfaced every time she was alone.

"I'm falling in love with her," she said to the ocean as a wave broke around her feet. "What shall I do?"

She had lost count of the times she had framed a sentence, rehearsed her story, preparing to tell Annabel about the money. But somehow the moment never seemed quite right. There was always some reason to put it off. Some excuse, Cody corrected. Coward, she thought angrily. It was not that she didn't trust Annabel — or was it?

When Margaret had left, Cody had felt the trust seep out of her, leaving a hollowness deep inside and a compulsion to protect herself. Now she had spent the past week exposing herself physically with an abandonment that shocked even her, yet all the while she knew she had been pushing Annabel away emotionally. She couldn't carry on like that if she wanted their relationship to have a chance. It was time she stopped hiding behind the excuse of the money secret and started being honest.

Cody paused and stared into the blue horizon. She knew then with absolute certainty what she had to do.

"I need to come into Rarotonga with you today," Cody announced over coffee.

A flutter of apprehension stirred Annabel's insides. "Fine," she said calmly. She resisted the urge to ask Cody why. Having sex with a woman did not mean owning her, and at the moment sex seemed to be all she did have with Cody.

A reticence surfaced in Cody every time she came too close, and Annabel had learned that confronting her only exacerbated the situation.

With unsteady fingers, she poured another strong Atiu coffee and wondered what Cody planned to do in Rarotonga.

Cody drained her cup and got to her feet. "I have to drop by home before we leave."

Annabel felt that familiar yearning in the pit of her stomach as she watched Cody slip into her sandals. She was wearing outrageously short shorts and a clinging white tanktop that emphasized the deep tan she had acquired since coming to the island. Her limbs were smooth and muscular and

Annabel was suddenly flooded with images of her naked, of the two of them entwined in fierce passion, of her face saturated with sweat and Cody.

Don't leave me, she implored wordlessly, then felt humiliated. She was becoming dependent. Sex addiction. It happened. And after all, she'd been celibate for more than a year before coming to the island. She thought grimly of her former adrenalin highs. She didn't need to repeat that addictive pattern in her relationships. It was destructive and ultimately unsatisfying. Short-term gratification, and that's all. Not that there was anything wrong with having sex for plain enjoyment, no strings attached. But she had already done that and she wanted more this time. She wanted to be close to Cody. She wanted that intense intimacy they experienced in lovemaking to extend to other levels.

But for that to be possible Cody had to trust her, and Annabel was beginning to despair of that ever happening. Sometimes she felt like grabbing Cody and shaking her, yelling at her that she wasn't the only one who was scared. That she didn't have the monopoly on unresolved grief, that nothing she was hiding could be any worse than some of Annabel's less appetizing exploits.

Cody came up, dropped a quick hard kiss on Annabel's mouth and said, "See you at the strip."

With two hours to kill before she had to turn up for the flight, Annabel decided to sort out once and for all why Aunt Annie had insisted that she come to Moon Island. She had allowed herself to become distracted by Cody over the past week and, if she was completely honest with herself, she had been secretly relieved to have an excuse to abandon those uncomfortable forays into her Aunt's private world. No matter how much she told herself that Aunt Annie wouldn't have written that letter if she hadn't wanted Annabel to do what she was doing, it still felt underhand and voyeuristic.

With reluctant fingers, she opened the 1959 diary where she had hurriedly closed it a week ago.

> *I am so fed up with this great big stomach and constant rushing to the bathroom. Rebecca is very patient with me, the dear angel. No matter how crotchety and unreasonable my demands, she is all tenderness. Sometimes I feel so frightened about having the baby and I hate the way my body is out of control. The doctor says I have only a week or so to endure this discomfort and I have certainly reached the stage where I shall sing and dance the day I feel my first pains. Rebecca has already engaged a nurse for the baby and we have chosen a list of names, all girls'!*

Annabel slid a bookmark into the diary and dropped it heavily onto her knee. Her heart was racing and she felt dizzy, a little nauseated. Aunt Annie had had a baby. She couldn't believe it. What had happened to the child? Was there a child?

Agitated, she began flicking through the pages to catch phrases, words.

> *... took so long ... weak ... The baby is so beautiful, the most beautiful baby in the*

world ... Rebecca is besotted ... we are
calling her Lucy ... leaving for Moon Island
tomorrow ... so tired but Lucy is a vision ...

The entire diary was full of Lucy. Lucy's first smile, sitting up, eating solids, starting to walk. Annabel's hands were shaking uncontrollably by the time she reached the final page and her whole body felt slippery with perspiration.

Lucy! She had never heard anyone mention a cousin. Born in 1959. They'd be the same age. Annabel felt momentary outrage, quickly followed by pain. She thought of her huge toy-filled bedroom, the inanimate playmates which had substituted for other children, the desperate loneliness of her growing up.

She had been painfully shy about her appearance from the time she was a small child and had first become conscious of her curiosity value. People never meant to be cruel. She had realized that eventually. But at the time their comments had forced the sensitive child she had been deep into a protective shell.

How different it would have been if she'd had a sister, a cousin, to grow up with. Lucy. Annabel bit her lip and located her Aunt's next diary. For a moment she sat just holding it, a curious heaviness settling on her chest. Then she opened it and read solidly until the sound of an engine intruded on her consciousness.

"Damn." She got to her feet and peered out the window. Then she walked resolutely into her kitchen and lifted the handpiece from her radio set.

ﻥ ﻥ ﻥ ﻥ ﻥ

"Annabel won't be coming," Bevan Mitchell informed Cody as soon as she arrived. "She asked me to let you know and to invite you to dinner with her when you get back."

Cody raised her eyebrows. "Thanks," she said stiffly and could not help but glance across her shoulder in the direction of Annabel's house.

Was she all right? It wasn't like Annabel to skip a day. Aware of an almost physical tugging sensation, she was momentarily tempted to abandon her plans and go straight back to Annabel's. But common sense got the better of her. If Annabel wasn't well or needed her, she would have said so. They weren't joined at the hip, Cody reminded herself brutally. She clambered aboard the Dominie telling herself to act maturely.

"Business in Rarotonga?" Bevan observed as he taxied the plane around to prepare for takeoff.

"A little." She caught his quizzical look, but wouldn't be drawn.

She managed not to scream or otherwise make a fool of herself during the flight, however she did gulp a much needed breath as they touched down.

"There. Not so bad now, was it?" Bevan pronounced with the confidence of a dentist extracting a tooth.

Cody grunted a response and refrained from kissing the ground.

"I'll see you back here at four then," he said as she headed for the terminal.

It took half an hour to buy a return ticket to Auckland.

"For tomorrow?" The agent seemed surprised and

Cody figured most people made their travel arrangements a little further in advance.

Bevan had said he wouldn't be long in Avarua as Smithy, his mechanic, had already picked up their fruit order. Restlessly, Cody watched a few tourists come and go, then decided she may as well return to the Dominie. The sooner they got back to Moon Island, the sooner she could see Annabel.

To her surprise, Bevan was already waiting when she got there, and he appeared to be stacking cargo in the hangar instead of the plane. With sudden unease, Cody approached.

"We won't be going back today," Bevan answered her unspoken question. "We have a slight problem with our fuel. There's water in it, and God knows what else." He rolled his eyes eloquently. "Someone forgot to clean the barrel out — who knows? It happens all the time."

Cody raised frantic eyes. "So what can we do? We *have* to get back today." She didn't add that her flight to New Zealand left the next morning.

"No chance." Bevan shook his head. "I have to drain the fuel lines, filter the damned stuff, and test-run the motors for at least half an hour. There's no way I can do all that before tomorrow lunchtime, especially with Smithy away today."

"Oh no!" Cody stamped her foot. "I don't believe this."

"I'll book you in at The Rarotongan," he told her. "And I'll give you a call tomorrow when she's mobile again."

"Damn it!" Cody exploded. "Can't I do something? I know a bit about motors." Her stormy eyes swept the length of silver plane. "I just *have* to get back to the island today, Bevan."

"I'm sorry Cody. Even if we could get her going today we'd be flying at night and there's no way we could land. You've seen the strip. There's not a single marking on it, much less lights."

Cody pulled a deep shaky breath. "I'm sorry. It's just that I'm leaving for New Zealand tomorrow morning and I needed to speak to Annabel before I go."

Bevan's face was impassive. "There's a pretty powerful short-wave transmitter here. We could try radioing her."

Cody gripped his arm. "Thank you. Yes! The radio!"

She hovered impatiently as Bevan signalled, ''Moon. Moon Radio. This is Dominie two-one-eight-five. Come in please. Come in Moon. Do you read me ... Repeat do you read me? Over."

There was nothing, just an occasional pulse of static. He tried again.

"She must be out of range," he noted. "Depends on the weather. I'll take you to the hotel then I'll give it another shot."

Cody hesitated, frowning at the radio set, then gave in. There didn't seem to be any alternative.

CHAPTER NINE

It was first light when Annabel finally stopped reading through letters and diaries, but the beauty of the new day was lost on her. Dazed, she went into the kitchen and mechanically brewed a pot of strong coffee.

Somewhere in the back of her mind she had registered something odd about yesterday and when her eyes strayed past the handset on her bureau, she remembered. The Dominie. She hadn't heard it return. It was possible that she'd been so absorbed she hadn't noticed the familiar throaty hum of the flyover, but she doubted it. Besides, Cody hadn't arrived for dinner and Annabel couldn't imagine her just not turning up.

With stiff fingers she poured a coffee and carelessly gulped down the hot liquid. She felt curiously numb, assailed by a sense of unreality. Her glance swept the living area, halting at a large photograph of Aunt Annie. Why? she asked wordlessly, then stalked out onto the verandah craving some fresh air. Her head felt foggy, filled with a crush of fragmented memories.

Her father. *Poor Ann ... more unstable by the year.*

Her mother. *Don't be so hard on her, Theo, she's had a difficult time.*

A "difficult time." Understatement of the year. Engaged to a man whose advances she detested and who had finally raped her, resulting in a pregnancy in — in Lucy. Annie had moved to Moon Island after the baby was born and for eighteen months she and Rebecca had lived in absolute bliss. Her diaries had so clearly documented her happiness, her absolute passion for Rebecca, the magic of their time together.

In 1961 Rebecca had reluctantly traveled to New York for her brother's wedding and to attend to what Annie had described as "family matters." Annie had wanted to accompany her, but Lucy had just recovered from a fever and the two women decided a sea voyage would be too difficult for the toddler.

Two months later Rebecca was killed in a car accident, only days before she was due to return. By the time Annie learned what had happened, her lover had already been buried.

Rebecca's family then contested her will, in which everything had been left to Annie. And they won, for Annie was so devastated she simply couldn't face a legal battle. Fortunately for her, the "family matters" Rebecca had mentioned had included transferring Moon Island and a substantial portion of her investments entirely into Annie's name, transactions uncannily completed in the week before her death.

Shattered, Annie had traveled back home to Boston. What happened there Annabel could only guess. Her aunt had left no diaries for the next five years, although Annabel had turned the house upside down, opened roll after roll of letters, skimmed through every subsequent diary. It was as though those five years didn't exist. And, worst of all, it was as though Lucy had disappeared off the face of the earth. The child was never mentioned again.

Annabel gazed into the glare of the morning, hands pressed to her throbbing temples. She felt choked, but unable to cry. She could remember times with her aunt, stilted conversations over dinner, her parents looking on with mask-like smiles and another emotion in their eyes. Anger? Fear?

Aunt Annie had once invited her to Moon Island, but she had been forbidden to go by her parents, and the invitation had not been repeated. On one of the rare occasions she had been alone with her aunt, Annabel could remember glowing with pleasure at her kind words, her support. They had talked for hours, Annabel confiding her worst fears about being shunned because of her appearance, about feeling unloved and unlovable. She remembered now what Annie had said. *Love is always there for us. But we*

have to look it in the face, expose ourselves.
Sometimes it's easier to hide.

As time went by, Annabel had developed a special bond with her aunt and had made it her business to see her as often as she could. Annie owned a home in San Francisco and had divided her time between that city and her beloved island.

After graduation, Annabel had become her aunt's frequent guest. It was Annie who had shared Annabel's grief over the breakup with Clare. Yet never once had she mentioned her own tragedy, her life with Rebecca, her child.

Annabel glanced about her and realized her feet had carried her automatically to Hibiscus Villa.

"Cody," she called. The door was locked. Annabel sat down on the verandah.

They must have stayed in Rarotonga for some reason. What if they hadn't? What if something was wrong? A wild panic gripped her. She was panting hard by the time she reached her house. Heart pounding, she radioed Bevan Mitchell.

The response was immediate. "Moon Radio. This is Dominie two-one-eight-five. I read you. Over."

"Where are you?" Annabel burst out. "Over!"

"At five hundred feet. Twelve o'clock high, Moon. Out."

Annabel slammed down the set and marched outside just in time to see the little plane circle her house and then carry on to the airstrip. Furious, she stalked back indoors, gathered up her riding gear and headed straight for Kahlo's stable.

* * * * *

114

"Where the hell have you been?" she greeted Bevan.

He pulled on his cigarette. "Now you don't think I'd gone and committed suicide out there, did you?"

Annabel bit her lip. She was behaving like an idiot. Distractedly she looked around. "Where's Cody?"

Bevan removed the cigarette and Annabel noticed him stiffen. "She left this morning," he said quietly.

"Left?" Annabel's mouth went dry.

"We tried to make radio contact with you yesterday and again this morning, but we couldn't raise you." He felt about in his shirt and produced a folded slip of paper. "She asked me to give you this."

Annabel stared down at it for a moment, then stuffed it into her pocket.

"She seemed upset," the pilot added carefully.

"Did she . . ." Annabel tried to frame a question.

"She was traveling back to New Zealand," Bevan told her. "That's all I know. I'm sorry."

Annabel gave him a nod then, on shaking legs, mounted Kahlo and reined her toward the beach. "I won't be coming tomorrow, Bevan," she told the pilot. "There are two guests to meet. Can you handle everything?"

"No problem." He lit up again. "I'll radio when we arrive."

With a brief wave of thanks, Annabel rode off.

Cody had gone. Right when she needed her. I've gambled and lost, Annabel reflected bitterly. It had probably been naive to expect any degree of commitment from someone who was still getting over the breakup of a long-term relationship.

Tears stinging, she headed for the sea and whipped Kahlo into a gallop, weaving in and out of the surf until she reached the familiar crescent of Passion Bay. She slowed only as they neared the track back to Villa Luna, and tethered Kahlo under the palms.

"I'll be back soon, girl." She patted the mare and strolled down toward the sea, reaching into her pocket for Cody's letter. It was empty.

Frowning, Annabel stuffed her hands into every other pocket, then ran frantically up the beach. The crumpled note she finally retrieved from the water's edge was soaked through. A wave flopped across her feet as she peeled it open. She stared in disbelief, then she tried to laugh. But the only sound that emerged was harsh sobbing.

Cody's writing was dispersed across the page in a mass of inky rivulets. Only the first line was legible.

I'm sorry Annabel. I wanted to tell you but ...

CHAPTER TEN

Cody woke up in a small crowded room, its windows wet with condensation, the sky beyond a lethargic grey. She gazed about then closed her eyes again, willing her surroundings to disappear. Janet was still asleep, her cheeks rosy and her long brown hair tumbling across the pillow. Looking at her best friend, Cody felt a rush of affection and wished for a moment that she could have fallen in love with Janet.

Life would have been so uncomplicated. Janet was calm, happy, a great cook and enthusiastic gardener. They liked the same music, movies and sports. Their backgrounds were similar and they lived in the same city. What more could a woman want?

Cody conjured up a vision of making love with Janet. It seemed to revolve around cuddling, and stroking her hair. It felt comforting instead of exciting. Cody stretched out an experimental finger and touched Janet's cheek, then wriggled a little closer so that she could put an arm around her.

Janet opened sleepy eyes, smiled at Cody happily and moved into her arms with a sigh of contentment. "I've missed you so much," she said and kissed Cody's cheek.

"I've missed you too, Janet." Cody gently kissed her mouth.

Their eyes met and Cody saw the uncertainty in Janet's, but she still slid her hand under her friend's pajama jacket and stroked her back. She felt so different from Annabel; she was smaller, softer. Cody continued her exploration and kissed her again.

"Cody!" Janet was pressing her hands flat against Cody's chest, pushing her away. "What are you doing?"

Cody's heart thumped and her head felt heavy. "I ..." she wavered. What indeed? "I want to make love to you," she said flatly.

Janet examined Cody's face. "Are you sure that's what you want?" she asked. "I mean, I *have* had more romantic propositions."

Cody frowned. "I ..." she began. "I ... Oh damn." She rolled restlessly onto her back and heaved a profound sigh. "Hell, I don't know, Janet. I'm sorry. I'm just being a schmuck."

Janet laughed. "Well I'm probably being the mug of the year. If it gets out I'll be a laughing stock at the club. The only dyke in Wellington who'd be fool enough to turn down Cody Stanton. Ever since word got round about you and Margaret the phone's been running hot with desperates offering me bribes to fix up a date with you."

"You're joking!" Despite herself, Cody grinned. "With me?"

"False modesty never did suit you," Janet said pertly. "If I could sell timeshares in your body, Cody Stanton, I'd be a rich woman."

She paused, pulled Cody into an embrace and kissed her sensually. "See," she said against Cody's mouth after a moment. "Nice, but ... nothing. Who is she?"

Cody stiffened, then met her friend's amused brown eyes candidly. "Her name is Annabel, Annabel Worth. And she ... we ..."

"I see," said Janet, with expressive eyebrows. "Tell me more."

Hours later Cody dialed the Personnel Manager at her ex-employer's and booked an appointment.

"Did you tell her?" Janet asked.

"No. I'd rather do it face to face. Besides, I wouldn't want to get there and find a paddy wagon waiting."

Janet laughed. "I suspect the boys in blue have better things to do, like maybe catching muggers and rapists."

Cody grinned back at her. "Let's do lunch."

"Can you afford it?"

"I have exactly one hundred, forty-two dollars and sixty cents to my name."

Both surveyed the neatly stacked banknotes lined up along the kitchen table and sighed audibly.

"Ninety thousand dollars," Janet said. "It doesn't look like much, does it?"

"Just a lot of paper," Cody said quietly.

ъ ъ ъ ъ ъ

Annabel paced her verandah restlessly, a glass of scotch in one hand and a cigarette in the other. She hadn't smoked in years and had coughed and spluttered for the first few drags. She'd found a half-full box in one of her Aunt's cupboards and figured they must have been left by a guest, or one of Annie's lovers, perhaps. In recent years Annie'd had a few too, Annabel recalled. Perhaps she had finally gotten over Rebecca.

It was three days since Cody had gone, and Annabel had given up wondering what else Cody's note had said. She had interrogated the staff at the Rarotongan, lied to Air New Zealand officials and stamped her foot in the Post Office. All she had managed to elicit was that Cody Stanton had left for Auckland, New Zealand. She had given no forwarding instructions for her mail and she had paid cash for her hotel room.

Annabel had deliberated over going to the police but, thinking of the poster, she held back. If Cody was in any kind of trouble the last thing Annabel wanted to do was make things worse for her.

As it happened she had little choice in the matter, for the police, finally discovering Cody had been on Moon Island, had contacted her. After offering condolences on the death of her Aunt — the donor of a sea rescue craft to the local station — the young sergeant had been remarkably forthcoming. He had even phoned his Wellington counterparts for more information.

"A relative, Miss Margaret Redmond, wishes to contact Miss Stanton," he explained to Annabel. "She believes Miss Stanton may be depressed, possibly suicidal. A family dispute it seems ..."

Annabel kept her face impassive. "Really? Margaret Redmond?" What was Cody's ex doing going to the police with a story like that?

"Evidently Miss Redmond said something about arranging a reconciliation," the officer enlarged.

Annabel felt the blood drain from her face. A reconciliation? That explained everything.

"So I guess there's nothing more for us to do now that Miss Stanton has returned home," he was going on. "I'll notify Wellington. Thanks for your help, Ms. Worth."

"It was a pleasure," Annabel had said, her voice heavy with irony.

The days that followed were a nightmare. Trying to force Cody out of her mind, Annabel had gone over her Aunt's diaries again, scouring for more clues about what had happened after Rebecca died. In her mind she constructed version after version of the truth.

Annie had got a job in Boston and Lucy had died tragically of some obscure illness ... Annie and Lucy had gone to live with relatives in Europe and Lucy had been killed in a second tragic accident ... Lucy's fever turned out to be meningitis and she had died soon after Annie reached Boston.

If only Cody had stayed, Annabel thought

distractedly as she stubbed out her cigarette. More than anything, she longed to discuss the whole mysterious business with someone else, gain another woman's perspective. There was something blindingly obvious that she was just not seeing. And somewhere in the back of her memory a faint chord registered, a phrase ran through her head over and over — *She need never know.*

Who had said that? Her brows knitted as fragments shifted in and out of focus. The letter Jessup had asked her about — addressed to "Lucy"; the uncanny sense of deja vu that had beset her ever since she set foot on the island; the missing diaries; the family silence around Annie's life and that of her child; Annabel's inheritance.

Annabel churned it over and over, poured another scotch, lit another cigarette. She was becoming obsessed. She had to stop thinking about it, creating a soap opera out of her life. *Pull yourself together,* she ordered sternly. Then she froze, choking on a mouthful of scotch. It hit her with such blinding clarity she couldn't credit that she hadn't seen it before.

"No," she whispered. It wasn't possible. It simply couldn't be.

But every cell in her body knew.

CHAPTER ELEVEN

Janet saw Cody off at the airport.

"Well you can't afford a taxi, can you?" she joked innocently.

Cody held her close and said, "I love you."

"Oh, Cody!" Janet clutched her friend. "I hope everything works out."

Cody hugged her closer. "Me too," she murmured. "I'll write." She handed Janet a tissue and waited for her to mop up, then bent to kiss her. "Bye sweetie," she said softly.

Cody slung her cabin bag over her shoulder and wandered out of the terminal and across to the cargo hangers. There was no sign of the Dominie and she checked her watch.

"You lookin' for someone?" A small weathered man in white overalls approached her.

"Yes, is Bevan Mitchell about?" she asked politely.

"Not 'ere," she was told. "Lad's gone 'ome. His mum passed on." Catching Cody's startled eyes, he added, "He didn't take the Dominie. She's still 'ere and I'm the mechanic." He wiped a hand on his overalls and held it out. "Name's Smith."

Cody shook it gingerly. "Pleased to meet you, Mr. Smith." She shot a quick uncertain look at the sky. "So, er ... who's flying the Moon Island shuttle then?"

"The lady 'erself. Miz Worth."

Cody blanched. "Annabel?" It came out more like a loud squeak than a question.

The mechanic nodded as though humoring the simple-minded. "Like I said. Miz Worth's been flying 'er the last few days. Cap'n Mitchell taught 'er, says she's a natural."

"A natural," Cody repeated dumbly. Born to fly. And Bevan had taught her. Bastard. The thought of Annabel flying that decrepit apology of a plane ...

The old mechanic was still rambling on in his thick cockney English. "Nothin' wrong with lady fliers Miss. 'Melia Earhart, Amy Johnson, Jean Batten an' the like ... Course Cap'n Mitchell said she weren't to fly on 'er own, but you know Miz

Worth." He seemed to laugh and cough all at once and Cody bit her lip nervously.

"Is she expected this afternoon?" she ventured.

"Guess so." He glanced up toward the sun. "Due any time, I'd say. You can rest yer bones over there." He indicated a small bench in the shade of the hanger. Fanning herself, Cody gratefully occupied it.

She didn't have to wait long before she detected the familiar whine of Bevan Mitchell's pride and joy. The little silver plane landed elegantly and taxied off the runway and over toward them. Cody watched the pilot jump out and her heart turned over. Annabel was wearing a thin silk shirt tucked into khaki pants and a rather battered bomber jacket. This she removed as the heat greeted her, but she kept on her dark glasses and thin leather flying gloves.

Cody could hear her talking to the English mechanic but couldn't make out a word they were saying. Annabel appeared to be indicating something on one wing and Smith was poring over the flap. She looked very assured, hands on hips, attention totally absorbed by the little plane. Then, as if she sensed she was being watched, she turned around and stared toward the hanger.

"Annabel!" Cody emerged, waved, hurried across the hot tarmac.

"Cody. Hi there," Annabel drawled softly. Cody flinched at the coolness in her tone. "Coming over?"

"Yes. If you'll take me."

"Sure. I've got to pick up a few supplies first," she said, business-like. "But I won't be long."

"I'll come with you, and give you a hand," Cody offered.

"Thanks," Annabel said cursorily. "But Smithy's coming into Avarua with me and I'm sure we can manage between us."

She sounded polite and disinterested and small shock waves rippled through Cody. She wished she could see Annabel's eyes but she hadn't removed her glasses. In fact she had barely glanced at Cody.

"Let's go, Smithy," she signaled the mechanic as she peeled off her gloves and tossed them into the Dominie. "Sit in the plane, if you wish," she told Cody in a flat tone. "But it's probably cooler where you were."

With that, she strolled off with the mechanic.

As they moved out of sight Cody rounded on the hapless Dominie and delivered a swift kick to its undercarriage. "Shit," she muttered. "Looks like you blew it, kid."

"I didn't know you could fly," Cody commented after they were safely off the ground and leveling off. Sitting next to Annabel, she was dazzled by her obvious control.

"Officially I can't, but these are the Cook Islands. It's no different from driving. It wouldn't matter if you were Niki Lauda, you'd still have to buy a local license and drive a cop from the police station to the roundabout and back, just to prove you know the difference between the brakes and the accelerator."

"Fascinating," said Cody with a hint of irony.

Annabel didn't seem to notice.

Cody tried again. "So how are you?"

"I'm fine. You?"

Cody's throat felt tight. "I'm fine, Annabel." She stretched out a hand, resting it on the warmth of Annabel's thigh. "You look stunning as a pilot," she told her truthfully.

Annabel didn't reply and Cody became aware of a tension in her body, a rejection of her touch. Self-consciously she withdrew her hand. "Is something wrong?" she asked shakily.

"Let's talk when we reach the island. I need to concentrate on getting us there in one piece."

The next hour was spent in silence, Annabel intent on her task, Cody trying to control her rising panic. She only had a few more days booked on the island, she thought with dismay. Annabel was obviously upset about something and Cody could only hope they would resolve it in what little time was available.

"Would you like to come up to Villa Luna for a coffee?" Annabel asked as she secured the plane after yet another perfect landing.

She could have been talking to a stranger, Cody thought miserably. But she accepted anyway and, lugging a box of supplies, followed Annabel's athletic figure through the palm trees. Annabel was obviously determined to keep her at a distance. What did it all mean?

"Annabel," she blurted the moment they entered the villa. "Is there someone else?"

Annabel halted. "I don't know. Is there?"

"For me?" Cody was confused. "Of course not!"

"So what the hell was it that sent you rushing back to New Zealand so fast you couldn't even say goodbye?" She stalked into the sitting room, Cody hot on her heels.

"Annabel! Didn't you read my note?"

"I would have. If you hadn't used a damned fountain pen."

Cody felt like some giant hand was squeezing her gut. "I don't understand," she said unevenly.

"It got wet. I was riding along the beach and it was in my pocket and . . ." Annabel started to pour herself a drink then slammed the bottle down. "Oh, what's the use? Even if I had read it, how do you think I'd have felt having you disappear on me like that?"

"It wasn't my fault the bloody Dominie broke down and I couldn't get back."

"Oh, and I suppose if you had, you'd have told me all about Margaret . . ." She trailed off, looking flushed.

"Margaret?" Cody's jaw dropped. "What are you talking about?"

Annabel folded her arms. "I'm talking about your reconciliation."

"Jesus, Annabel!" Cody flung herself onto the settee. "I haven't laid eyes on Margaret since the day she walked out on me. Where the blazes did you get that idea?"

Annabel crossed the room and located a sheet of paper. "Here." She thrust it at Cody.

Cody scanned the flyer. "Where did you get this?"

"The police," Annabel said. "They told me 'family' were trying to get hold of you for a reconciliation. And when I asked, the family turned out to be one Margaret Redmond."

Cody stared down at her own face and nearly cried with relief. A wanted poster. Her worst nightmare. And it had nothing to do with the money. She wiped a hand weakly across her forehead and shook her head.

"I went back to New Zealand to sort out some urgent business, Annabel," she said quietly. "It had nothing to do with Margaret. I hope you believe me." She reached out and took Annabel's hand. "Oh Annabel. I was so upset about not getting back to the island that day and I have such a lot to tell you. I want us to spend every minute of this week together."

Annabel stiffened. "I'm afraid that won't be possible." Her voice was tight and still a little distant. "You see, I'm flying back home tomorrow. I didn't know what was going on with you and I need to go ... so ..."

"Home?" Cody whispered. "Home, as in Boston?"

"That's right." Annabel pulled free of Cody and moved across to the liquor cabinet to pour herself a drink. "Like you, I have some urgent business to attend to."

She sipped at a scotch and Cody watched her through narrowed eyes. She'd never seen Annabel drink in the afternoon and as much as she tried to tell herself it was none of her affair, it bothered her. The "urgent business" was obviously a stressful subject and Cody sensed Annabel was in no mood to discuss it.

"When will you be back?" she asked, trying not to sound like she was pressuring her.

"I don't know. It depends on what happens. At this stage I haven't booked a return." She sounded off-hand, as though she couldn't care less whether she came back.

Cody felt cold. That couldn't be true. She knew it

wasn't. Maybe Annabel was applying for a job, she speculated. Or was there a woman, after all? Cody got to her feet. "Annabel, last week you said you wanted something more than a holiday fling with me," she reminded her. "I want that too. That's why I did what I did. To clear up a few problems back home so I could concentrate on us."

She stood in front of Annabel and deliberately took the drink out of her hand. Annabel raised shuttered eyes and Cody had the impression that she had somehow walled herself round with glass. Her body exuded control, tension — and her face was a cool, detached mask.

Cody trailed a finger down her cheek and across her bottom lip, feeling an involuntary response there. She stretched her hand around the back of Annabel's neck and soothed the taut muscles with gentle fingers. "You're beautiful," she said, pulling Annabel to her feet. She felt Annabel's resistance and tried not to be hurt by it. She couldn't believe Annabel had gone cold on her over a silly poster and a misunderstanding. There had to be something else. And whatever it was, it had deeply disturbed her.

Wanting to comfort her — and also just plain wanting her — Cody slid her arms around Annabel's waist and pulled her close, shivering slightly at the memory of her body.

"Cody, I ..." Annabel began, but Cody covered her mouth with her own and kissed her gently.

She could feel the resistance draining out of Annabel's body, and smiled against her mouth. "Sssh," she whispered. "We can talk later."

She kissed her again, this time more passionately, and felt her mouth tremble open. Their tongues met delicately then Cody tasted salt. She opened her eyes and saw that Annabel was crying.

"Annabel," she said softly, kissing her neck. "Honey, what's wrong? I wish you would tell me."

Annabel shook her head and stretched her arms up around Cody's neck to pull her closer and Cody felt passion erupt through her body. Annabel's skin was hot and smooth under the silk of her shirt and Cody's hands caressed their way across her back and around to cup her breasts. She took a step back to slowly remove the shirt, absorbing Annabel's milky tautness with a candor that made the other woman's skin prickle in response.

"Cody," she whispered as Cody grazed a nipple with her teeth then nibbled delicately at the flesh of her stomach.

"You like this, Annabel?" Cody murmured between bites and proceeded to divest Annabel expertly of her trousers.

Annabel sighed and twisted Cody's T-shirt impatiently, then gasped as fingers slid under the silk of her cami-knickers to tease their way along her labia. She snatched Cody's hand away then and pulled her toward the bedroom, dragged off her T-shirt with impatient hands and threw it on the floor.

"Yes I like it," she said thickly, squirming as Cody's fingers found her clitoris through the damp silk. Cody was removing the rest of her clothes and Annabel opened her eyes to take in her nakedness; the well-defined muscles in her arms and shoulders, her dark tan, the hollows and curves that were still so new to her.

A sudden rush of feeling made her mouth

tremble and her heart race. She wanted to hold Cody and never let her go. Cody was easing them both back onto the bed, her fingers sliding Annabel's knickers out of the way, her mouth lightly tasting Annabel's.

They lay facing each other for a long moment, Cody' face oddly serious as she read the wanting in Annabel's. "We don't have to make it hard for ourselves, Annabel," she murmured. She gently took one of Annabel's hands and with small butterfly kisses caressed the palm, the fingertips, the wrist. Then she guided it with her own to sample the wetness between Annabel's legs.

"See," she said softly. "You feel exquisite." She pulled the hand back to her mouth and slowly licked the juices off Annabel's fingers and gathered her close.

As the minutes went by, a breeze stirred the palms like the rustle of a ballgown and the late sun filtered through the crystals in Annabel's window to cast rainbows across them. Shadows deepened, birds returned home and, as night fell, the moon turned the ocean silver.

Cody stirred in Annabel's arms, but was too soundly asleep to hear love whispered, or to feel Annabel's soft weeping.

CHAPTER TWELVE

"Annabel, darling. What a surprise." Laura Adams Worth moved forward and pecked the air next to Annabel's cheek.

"You look well, Mother," Annabel observed.

Thin and elegant in a pale linen dress and single strand of pearls, Laura never seemed to age. All her life Annabel could remember her mother looking like this: poised, expensive, and as distant as a Cape Cod horizon. The smell of her perfume brought memories rushing back and Annabel felt suddenly gauche, clumsy, unattractive: a stuttering eight year old tasting blood as braces gouged into her gums; a fifteen year old filled with shame when her period leaked at Thanksgiving and her mother had called in the maid to remove the gory chair.

Even now she could feel Laura Worth's critical blue eyes rejecting as crass and juvenile her choice of black tights, pink slingbacks and huge pink T-shirt.

Why did she do it? Annabel wondered. Whenever she visited her parents, some strange perversity made her pass over the respectable clothes that dominated her wardrobe in favor of those she knew her mother would most deplore. Childish attention-getting. Annabel knew that. Petty underground gameplaying. No wonder her therapist drove a Mercedes.

"Tea, my dear?" Her mother was already calling Doris, their Filipino maid.

Annabel nodded resignedly and flopped down onto a pristine peach leather sofa she'd never seen before. Obviously Laura still enjoyed a symbiotic relationship with her decorator. "Where's Daddy?"

"Playing golf," Laura replied without a flicker of interest. "In Newport. I'm not expecting him back all week."

"I guess I'll miss him then." Annabel felt a faint disappointment. At least she shared a few interests with her father. They could talk Wall Street, politics and horseflesh. And Theodore Worth made no secret of the fact that he worshipped his daughter. Not once had Annabel even been made to feel guilty for not being a son. Her father had taken her everywhere, taught her to trade stocks while she was still at prep school, put her at the helm of his yacht almost before she could walk and insisted she work at McDonald's on her vacations even though her mother acted as if Annabel were selling herself on Times Square.

Annabel had always sensed an ally in her father and the thought of facing her mother without him distressed her. She pressed her clammy hands together and, suppressing a wayward urge to ask for milk, watched Laura pour the tea and add a curl of lemon to each cup.

"Are you enjoying Anne's island, dear?" Laura asked.

"It's beautiful." Annabel sipped her perfectly brewed tea.

Laura was avoiding her eyes. "I hope you've placed Anne's affairs in the hands of competent people," she observed with a hint of censure.

"I've retained Aunt Annie's lawyer," she said trying not to sound defensive.

Her mother lifted a lightly penciled eyebrow. "Really, Annabel? I had never suspected you of sentimentality, my dear." She gave a short brittle laugh and looked at Annabel with a patronizing expression. "And I take it the urbane Mr. Jessup is still in good health?" she inquired facetiously.

Clearly Walter Jessup had prepped at the wrong school. She promptly decided to keep him on — so long as he could produce a female partner, that was.

"He sends his regards," she said coolly. "And this . . ." She reached into her satchel and dropped an envelope on the occasional table in front of her mother. It was the one addressed to Lucy.

135

"Aunt Annie left this with him, but Mr. Jessup hasn't been able to trace this person. I wondered whether you might have some idea who she is."

Laura glanced down at the envelope then looked at Annabel without blinking. "Lucy?" she toyed with the name. "No, I don't."

"I'm surprised," Annabel commented dryly. "I would have thought you might know the whereabouts of your niece."

Laura returned her cup to its saucer with a clatter and one hand strayed jerkily to her pearls. Annabel was certain she detected a flicker of emotion in her mother's light blue eyes. Fear? Guilt perhaps?

"What do you know about Lucy?" she asked Annabel tightly.

"That's what I'm asking you, Mother."

Laura Worth deposited her tea on the table, crossed her legs and regarded Annabel with assessing eyes. "Of course!" she said with a slight flutter. "I had all but forgotten. Poor little Lucy ..."

She shook her head sadly and Annabel felt suddenly insecure, as though she were walking on quicksand, her reality as insubstantial as a mirage. "Poor Lucy?" she queried.

Laura seemed to relax a little. "Anne's child," she explained. Lowering her head, she folded poignant hands in her lap. "A tragic business, absolutely tragic. Anne made me promise never to tell a soul, but ..." She eyed the envelope meaningfully, and Annabel immediately felt like a jerk.

Her mother's message was loud and clear. Laura was being asked to dishonor a promise — and to a dead woman. How could Annabel be so insensitive?

"Mother, I know Aunt Annie had a baby after she called off her engagement. And I know she lived with that child and a woman called Rebecca on Moon Island until Rebecca was killed. Then she came to Boston, didn't she?"

Laura paled and Annabel saw her hands were no longer folded but had balled into two tight fists.

"How do you know this, Annabel?" she asked with a hunted expression.

"Aunt Annie left me a letter and —"

"Anne told you!"

There was no mistaking her mother's agitation. Annabel felt her pulse begin to race. "I know a great deal about Aunt Annie," she said quietly, and watched dull red wash Laura's porcelain features.

Her mother rose and moved across the large room to stare out at her gardens, hands gripping the window ledge. "Anne did not want to have a baby," she said in a strained voice.

"Hardly surprising under the circumstances," Annabel retorted, recalling Annie's desperation about the rape.

"She had the baby in the Back Bay house," her mother went on as though she hadn't heard. "It was a difficult birth. She was very weak. Afterward she and ... Rebecca ... stayed for a short time then left for the island and —"

"What was she like?" Annabel interrupted.

"Who, the baby?"

"No. Rebecca."

Her mother stiffened. "She was a Gardner, the shipping people. Anne met her at college and they became close friends. Rebecca was such a wild girl ..."

Annabel could almost hear it. *Led poor Annie astray, turned her head.*

"After college Rebecca went to Europe. She fancied herself an artist." Laura frowned and her lips compressed. "Anne followed her over and ... Oh she was such an innocent and Rebecca's crowd was very bohemian ..."

"They became lovers?" Annabel translated boldly.

Her mother shuddered. "Father became very ill at that stage and Anne had the good sense to return home. After a few months she became engaged to Roger Lawrence, a very nice Harvard boy. He's a surgeon now, of course," she added with a sigh.

"Of course," said Annabel. "Specializing in gynecology, no doubt."

The acid jibe appeared to go straight past her mother. "She broke off the engagement quite suddenly, for no apparent reason."

"She was raped," Annabel said succinctly.

"Annabel!" Laura Worth looked outraged. "Roger was her fiance. He loved her."

"Funny way of showing it."

"You know nothing of these matters," her mother went on indignantly. "Anne was a highly-strung girl. She had little understanding of adult emotions. Roger certainly wasn't to blame for mistaking her reticence for the natural shyness of an inexperienced young woman."

Annabel gasped. It was plain that her mother was determined to cling to a sanitized explanation of what had really occurred between Annie and her Harvard fiance.

"Of course we tried to change her mind," she

continued, ignoring Annabel's disgust. "But she simply couldn't see what a mistake she was making."

Annabel rolled her eyes. "I doubt she was ever permitted to forget it."

Laura frowned but continued her story. She seemed almost relieved and Annabel guessed she must have been holding on to enormous resentment, bottling up a family secret like this over the years.

"Then she found she was expecting." Her mother lowered her voice, her mouth tightening into a thin straight line. "She had already written to Rebecca it seems, and within a month they had set up house together. Anne refused to see Roger at all and insisted he be told the child was not his. The poor boy nearly went out of his mind."

Annabel snorted under her breath. "So in the end Annie and Rebecca took the baby Lucy back to Moon Island, and that's where they lived."

"Yes," Laura said. "We didn't see the child again until that dreadful accident."

"By which time presumably I was a toddler?"

Laura Worth nodded, her eyes distant and focused somewhere beyond Annabel's shoulder. Her expression made Annabel uneasy.

"So what happened when they came back to Boston?" she prompted.

Her mother turned to stare out the window for a long moment. "Anne was very depressed," she said dully. "She simply refused to speak with anyone, even the child. Poor little Lucy. She was just a baby."

Annabel's eyes widened. She could have sworn there was genuine emotion in her mother's voice.

Laura had folded her arms and was pacing absently back and forth across the garden view. "She stayed like that for months, silent and wasting away. We tried everything, had her seen by experts. They prescribed drugs but Anne would not take them. She refused to help herself at all."

She sounded unreasonably angry and Annabel suddenly wondered what it must have been like for Laura, the competent organizer and perfect young Boston matron, having to cope with a younger sister's despair. Despair over a *lesbian* lover . . .

"In the end we were desperate."

"Desperate?" Annabel echoed.

"Yes." A defensive note. "We decided that Anne would benefit most from full-time psychiatric care."

"You put her in a mental hospital?" Annabel asked slowly.

Her mother lowered her head and suddenly Annabel noticed her age; the stoop of her shoulders, the chin sagging slightly. "We did what we thought was best," she said tiredly.

"And Lucy?"

There was a long pause. Annabel tried to read her mother's expression, but her eyes were veiled, her face mask-like.

"Lucy became unwell and died." It was said blankly and something in her tone jarred. Annabel felt the hairs on the back of her neck prickle.

"Lucy died," she repeated matter-of-factly. "Then why did Aunt Annie leave this for her?" She lifted the envelope and her mother flinched.

"Anne was disturbed," Laura said quietly. "When she came out of hospital she said she didn't want to talk about Rebecca or Lucy ever again. She was not herself."

Annabel watched her mother carefully, recognizing that there was something not being said. "How long was Aunt Annie in the hospital?"

"Nearly five years," Laura said slowly.

"Five years?" Annabel got to her feet and stalked across the room to face her mother. "You let her stay there for five years!"

"Annabel!" her mother protested.

Annabel was enraged, fiercely, blindly angry. She took her mother by the arm and spun her around. "Why?" she demanded.

Laura shook her head dumbly.

"Was that the big white house we used to visit?" Fragments of a memory danced before Annabel. High spiked iron gates and a curving driveway, vacant-eyed strangers wandering across the lawns. She was never allowed outside to play and had to sit in a hot room filled with plants while her parents sipped tea with Aunt Annie. She had thought it was her Aunt's home.

"Oh my God," she whispered.

"You don't understand," Laura began, but Annabel was not listening.

"You kept her in a mental hospital while you raised her daughter!" she shouted, tightening the grip on her mother's arm and shaking her slightly.

Laura's face drained chalk white. "No . . ." she gasped. "Lucy died . . ."

"Don't lie to me, Mother," Annabel spat. "I want to know the truth. You owe me that much and you owe Annie."

"Annabel darling. Please don't ..." Laura's voice wavered on a sob and Annabel could feel her trembling.

Somewhere in the back of her mind Annabel was deeply shocked at her own behavior — shouting at her mother, handling her roughly. This was not what she'd planned at all. Somehow she had imagined ... What? A civilized little chat? She produces the envelope and Laura immediately pours out the truth after thirty years of secrecy? This was real life, she reminded herself. And feeling angry and frustrated still didn't give her the right to use her mother as a psychological punching bag.

Laura was crying openly, and with shattering clarity Annabel realized that it was the first time she had ever seen her mother show such emotion. Ashamed, Annabel released her grip and instead placed a tentative arm around the older woman's hunched shoulders.

"I'm sorry, Mom," she said huskily.

Laura covered her face with her hands. "I can't tell you," she sobbed. "I don't know how to begin."

"It's all right." Annabel led her to a settee and sat down beside her. "I love you, Mom," she said, and felt a profound shudder move her mother's body.

Laura looked up, her eyes pain-filled. "Lucy was such a beautiful little girl," she began and Annabel took her hand, pressing it encouragingly.

"She was an angel. She loved everyone and everything. The moment I first saw her I knew she was special. Anne was barely conscious during the birth and Rebecca was concentrating only on her. So the doctor gave Lucy to me and I held her and I ..." She began to cry again. "I loved her. Then they left and I didn't see her again until the accident."

She looked at Annabel with eyes that were suddenly soft and loving and Annabel felt her own tears begin.

"By then I had lost four babies of my own, stillborn or miscarried. And I saw Lucy so healthy and beautiful, and I felt bitterly envious of Anne. It seemed so unfair. I had done everything right. I'd married Theo, I kept myself fit and ate properly, took vitamins. And Anne had behaved scandalously her whole life and even lived with a woman ... as husband and wife ..." She blew her nose indelicately into a fine lace handkerchief, then tossed the sodden thing onto the floor.

"You can't have any idea how empty my life felt," she said brokenly. "I felt like a nothing. There seemed no point to my existence. All I was any good at was bridge, and I found it hard to convince myself that playing cards was the full extent of God's divine plan for my life."

She gave a watery smile and Annabel smiled back and gave her shoulders a squeeze. "I understand more than you think," she said softly, remembering the mindlessness of her life until she left for Moon Island.

Laura met her eyes and seemed to take strength from the genuine support she saw there. "When they came home after the accident I just didn't know what to do. Anne was beside herself, inconsolable. She said she didn't want to live without Rebecca." She paused, a haunted expression in her eyes. "They were so much in love, you see."

Annabel nodded. She knew from Annie's diaries how all-consuming that passion had been, even till the day she died. Her final entry bore stark testimony ... *My love, my love. At last together again ...*

"Poor Lucy. Anne hardly responded to the child and Lucy would forever run about the house searching under chairs and covers. When I asked her what she was doing she would say, 'Looking Becca'. I tried to comfort her and took her everywhere with me. Theo wanted to engage a nanny but I refused. I wanted her all to myself. I didn't deliberately take her away from Anne." She clutched at Annabel's hands with sudden desperation. "You must believe me."

Annabel stroked her hands soothingly. "Of course I believe you," she said through her own tears.

"Then Anne tried to kill herself and she had to go to a hospital. The doctors told Theo she needed psychiatric help but when we found out what was involved, we were horrified. Naturally we refused. But then she stopped speaking even to Lucy. It was as if she had gone away into another world and had just left her body behind. I used to put Lucy on her knee and she would play with Anne's big gold locket ..."

"I remember ..." Annabel said sickly and again the image flashed before her.

But this time she could see the face.

Annie's face.

Annie, her mother.

"In the end we met a young doctor, a woman. She had heard about Anne from a colleague and asked if she could examine her. She was very frank with us and revealed herself as a woman who was ... like Anne."

"She was a lesbian?" Annabel put in dryly.

"Yes. She was a lesbian," Laura repeated. Annabel knew what it must have cost her even to say that.

"She took Anne to Belletara, a private clinic. It was only meant to be for a week but Anne stayed."

"And Lucy?"

"We visited Anne most weekends and Theo and I treated Lucy like our own daughter. As time went by she started to call us Mommy and Daddy and it became very easy to forget that we weren't really her parents."

"So Lucy didn't die?" Annabel pressed, even though she knew the truth. She needed to hear it.

Laura shook her head slowly. "No. She thrived. Oh, Annabel ... I tried not to love her, become too attached, but when Anne asked us whether we would consider adoption, I was ecstatic."

"Annie asked you?" Annabel's mouth went dry.

"It was after a year. She said she didn't think she could raise Lucy and she had no idea when she would feel ready to leave the clinic. Theo took over her affairs along with Rebecca's lawyer, Maisie Jessup of San Francisco ... that's her son you deal with," she said as an aside. "We made all the arrangements and ..."

"Why did you change my name?" Annabel asked tightly.

Laura looked slightly ashamed. "We were frightened ... I was frightened. Roger, your natural father, knew of your existence under the name Lucy and he had inquired after you when Anne first arrived."

"So you made Lucy vanish?"

Her mother nodded. "Annabel was your second name."

Annabel sighed deeply and sagged back into the couch. "Why?" she said after a moment. "Why didn't you tell me?"

Laura Worth looked oddly calm, her body more relaxed than Annabel had seen it for years.

"I wanted to but I couldn't," she said simply. "At first I told myself it was to protect you, so you wouldn't feel abandoned. Then, when Anne finally discharged herself, we made an agreement never to tell you. That was my doing. You see, I was so terrified that Anne would come and claim you back. I never stopped being terrified all through the years. Sometimes I was almost too frightened to love you, in case you were snatched away from me ..." She looked at Annabel sadly and Annabel remembered with deep grief the coldness, the way her mother had kept her distance.

"I thought you didn't love me," she said quietly.

Laura blanched. "Oh Annabel. If only you knew. I feel so angry with myself now. When you live a lie it's like digging a grave. The longer you dig the deeper it gets until you can't climb out any more, even if you wanted to. In the end you find you've buried yourself."

She paused and shivered. "I tried to find a way to tell you when you were older, but even then I was too cowardly. I thought that if you found out you would leave me and go to Anne, that you would hate me ... and I couldn't bear that."

Annabel's heart thumped painfully. "I don't hate you," she said very gently. "How could I? I love you too much."

"Oh, Annabel." Her mother moved toward her and they clasped each other tightly.

Hours later, when she felt much calmer, Annabel opened the letter to Lucy.

My darling daughter,

I wish I could be with you as you read this. Now that you understand my life, can you also understand that I've always, always loved you.

Your mother,
Annie

CHAPTER THIRTEEN

"Moon. Moon Radio. Dominie two-one-eight-five at two thousand feet. Four miles southwest. Do you read me? Dominie to Moon. Come in please. Over."

She would never get used to the conventions of radio communication, Cody thought as she lifted the handset. "This is Cody," she said. "Um . . . over."

"Company on its way," said Bevan Mitchell. Cody's heart leaped. Annabel! "ETA fourteen hundred hours. Can you meet us? Over."

"I sure can. Fourteen hundred hours. That's

now!" Cody sprinted to the window to see if she could spot the Dominie.

"Five minutes, Moon," Bevan said but Cody was no longer listening. She was grabbing her hat and shades and frantically shoving cushions back into their usual places. As she ran out the door she heard Bevan's voice crackling over the radio but didn't bother to wait. All she could think about was his passenger.

"Margaret!" Cody's lips felt like they'd just been shot full of Novocaine.

"Cody. Hi!" Margaret threw herself into the arms Cody had stretched out to receive a box of pineapples. The fruit rolled haplessly around the tarmac while Bevan lit a cigarette and looked on with a cryptic expression.

Cody detached herself as quickly as she decently could and said weakly, "Well ... um ... what a surprise."

Margaret grinned. "A nice one I hope," she said looking Cody up and down. Then she whistled softly. "Sweetheart! You're looking real cute."

At that Bevan's jaw dropped visibly and his cigarette wavered in its groove. Cody cringed and backed away awkwardly. Clearly the presence of a man meant nothing to Margaret.

"You're staying on the island?" She asked the obvious while she gathered her wits.

"For two whole weeks," Margaret enthused. "Isn't that great, darling?"

Cody could scarcely believe what she was hearing. Numbly she took the bags Bevan tossed down.

"Manage those?" he queried dryly and Cody gave a quick, somewhat desperate nod. "I'll store the supplies then," he said.

Cody thanked him and turned to Margaret with a stoic expression. "Have you got your booking slip?" Margaret produced a voucher. "Hibiscus Villa," Cody read aloud with a sinking heart. Margaret would be five minutes walk from Luna Villa.

As they followed the trail Cody became increasingly alarmed. Alarmed at her sense of disorientation, her feeling that she barely knew this woman. Was it really Margaret? She stole a look. Same short, curly auburn hair, same laughing eyes and wide mouth, same voluptuous body — large breasts, narrow waist. This was Margaret, the woman she'd lain with for nearly five years, whose body she knew pore by pore.

"Where's Scott?" she asked abruptly as they turned into the clearing around Hibiscus Villa.

Margaret stopped in her tracks, looked up at Cody, and smiled her most seductive smile. "That's all over, Cody," she said softly.

Cody felt oddly queasy. She opened the villa and all but shoved Margaret in. The place reminded her unbearably of Annabel and she marveled at the sick joke fate had just played by sending Margaret instead. She felt tears prick and Margaret must have mistaken her obvious emotion for something else, for she hurried forward, pulling Cody into a hungry embrace.

"Oh, Cody, my darling," she whispered urgently.

"I've been desperate to see you. I feel like such a fool."

Her small hands were making circles on Cody's back and Cody felt her skin prickle in response. Then Margaret was kissing her and to Cody it was like being jerked back in time. They were lovers. It was a hot afternoon. Her body remembered every sensation. The sweat, the taste of Margaret's mouth, a clock ticking on her dresser, the roar of a plane overhead.

"Oh, Cody, I've missed you so much," Margaret was saying.

With a jolt Cody realized she was being undressed. She caught Margaret's hands and drew back, watching puzzlement alter her ex-lover's features. "What do you mean, it's all over with Scott?" she asked.

Margaret rolled expressive eyes. "The whole thing was a disaster. The moment we started living together he started ignoring me and acting like he had ownership papers. He was so unreasonable, Cody. He even expected me to go on the pill . . . can you believe that? He said condoms ruined the aesthetic, he —"

"Please!" Cody stopped her. "Spare me the gory details."

Margaret had the grace to look embarrassed. "Look, Cody," she said. "I know you're upset but this experience has been really important for me. It's really helped me resolve confusion about my sexuality."

"You were confused during our relationship?" Cody asked, dazzled by this new information.

"I know I should have told you sooner," Margaret

said quickly. "But I felt so guilty about being attracted to men. And I just kept on rationalizing it. You know, het conditioning and all that. But when I gave myself permission to explore those feelings without guilt-tripping myself, when I let go of buying into all that political crap — well, I really got to know myself."

"I'm happy for you," said Cody without expression.

Margaret seemed encouraged by this. "I found out that it's perfectly okay to have feelings for men as well as women. We're all one human race, after all. And my rebirther says that if we reject our feelings for men we reject the male in ourselves."

"The male in ourselves," Cody repeated. "And is your rebirther a dyke?"

Margaret looked puzzled. "No," she said. "Although she's very woman-oriented."

"Obviously," Cody commented.

She felt stunned. Right under her nose Margaret had been pining after men — *plural* — and feeling confused about her sexuality. Had she been blind, Cody wondered, or just plain stupid?

"So how do you feel about all this now?" she inquired.

Margaret smiled fulsomely. "I'm really at peace," she said. "I feel really connected to myself. I've accepted who I am and I don't care what society thinks."

"Lesbian and proud, eh?" Cody said.

Margaret looked a little taken aback. "No, bisexual, Cody. Bisexual and proud."

Cody took a deep breath and studied the woman in front of her, taking in the subtle changes she had missed at first. Margaret was thinner, her hair redder than usual and growing out of the close-cropped style she had always worn. She was wearing light-pink cotton knit pants and a designer T-shirt with a greenie slogan. Her nails were painted the same dark pink as her pants and her blue eyes looked heavy in her small face, mascara-caked very slightly in the fine creases beneath them.

"Why have you come here?" Cody finally asked.

Margaret's eyes widened in mute appeal. "To see you of course," she said in a hurt, little girl voice that once upon a time would have quickened Cody's pulse. "I've been trying to track you down for weeks. I even went to the police."

"So I gathered," Cody said dryly.

Margaret tugged at her arm, wetting her lips with the tip of her tongue. "Please don't be angry at me," she wheedled.

Cody took an automatic step back. "I'm not angry," she said. It was true. Looking at Margaret she felt absolutely nothing.

Her answer appeared to please Margaret who promptly grabbed her around the waist and pressed into her body. "I knew you'd forgive me," she sighed. "I was worried about that when I first spoke to Janet. She was really unhelpful even when I explained how important it was." She looked up at Cody as though expecting a supportive comment. Cody remembered that Margaret had always been jealous of her deep friendship with Janet.

"I asked Janet to keep my whereabouts a secret," Cody said. "I knew *she* could be trusted." She tried not to add the emphasis, but it slipped out anyway.

Margaret looked hurt. "You are still angry with me, aren't you?"

Cody put some distance between them by going into the kitchen for a glass of water. She felt as if she were talking to a stranger. Couldn't Margaret hear herself? Didn't she have any idea how Cody must have felt during this voyage of "self-discovery"? What it must have been like, after five years of living together, to have your lover walk out for a man she'd only just met? And now she was hearing their entire relationship reduced to little more than youthful experimentation for a woman confused about her sexuality!

"Christ, Margaret!" she spat. "What in hell did you expect? That I would be waiting around for you, desperate for whatever crumbs you might toss me? That you could kick me in the teeth, shit on my feelings and come crawling straight back when the bubble burst?"

Margaret had gone quite pale, her flirtatious looks replaced by a cautious, darting stare. She studied her hands miserably. "I thought you cared about me," she mumbled.

Cody deposited her glass on the bench with a restrained thud. "I did," she said, gritting her teeth. "I'm not the one who walked out, remember? I'm not the one who lied and manipulated."

Margaret leaned against the door jamb, twisting her T-shirt in her hands. "But I explained everything," she flared. "I told you I needed some space. I told you I was confused about my feelings for Scott."

"So you call leaving me and moving in with him getting some space?" Cody shouted.

Margaret put a hand to her mouth and looked beseeching. "I don't like it when you shout," she said. "My rebirther said that as long as I was completely true to myself, those who really loved me would support me. She said it would be cosmically impossible for anyone else to be hurt. She said I had to truly let go of my destructive patterns around men and —"

Cody raised her hands. "I don't believe this! I don't believe what I'm hearing. *My rebirther says. . .*" she parroted. "When are you going to switch your brain back on, Margaret? Your fucking rebirther is charging you fifty bucks an hour to stop you from thinking for yourself!"

"Cody!" Margaret lifted martyred eyes. "I'm finding this conversation very negative. I'm feeling very unsupported by you."

"Unsupported!" Cody laughed harshly. "Give me a break! I didn't ask you to come out here and I'm not interested in playing a whole lot of games with you. For God's sake you haven't even acknowledged how much you hurt me — said you're sorry . . . nothing."

"I know that all of this has brought up unresolved stuff for you, Cody, and I'm truly sorry if that process has been painful. I know you felt abandoned when your parents divorced and your brother died. I acknowledge that. But my re . . . I think it's really important that we take responsibility for our own stuff, not other people's."

"Oh I get the picture," Cody said coldly. "You decide our relationship is finished, so you're free to run after some toyboy. And if I feel terrible about that, it's because of *my* old stuff and has nothing to do with you. How convenient for you."

"This conversation is getting us nowhere," Margaret said, folding her arms stiffly.

"I wonder why that is?"

Cody's voice dripped sarcasm but Margaret didn't seem to notice. "You're just not hearing me," she said self-righteously. "If you loved me you would understand my point of view and support me."

Cody rolled her eyes. "Bullshit!" She met Margaret's gaze squarely. "I'm hearing exactly what you're saying and I won't even waste my time saying how despicable I find it. You don't need me to support your behavior. You've got your rebirther and your boyfriend, not to mention the church, the state and society at large. Cut the crap and be honest with yourself for a change, Margaret. You want all the emotional goodies you can get from women and to fuck with blokes at the same time. Call it bisexual if you like — after all it's very trendy, isn't it? Just don't expect me to stand back and applaud."

Margaret flushed dull red and glared at Cody, then that old sparkle lit her eyes. "You're beautiful when you're angry," she said with a giggle.

Cody looked at her incredulously. "Margaret," she said seriously, "I'm not going to bed with you, not now, not ever. I'm not in love with you any more." Even as she said it she was aware of a heady relief, a lightness in her heart. She didn't hate Margaret. She cared for her still. But the Margaret standing in front of her was not the woman she had loved.

"Is there someone else?" Margaret said dully.

"No," Cody corrected. "There is *someone* though."

"I see," Margaret said, examining her nails. "Your broken heart recovered pretty quickly, it seems."

Cody's temper flared. "Let's say knowing you'd left me to live with your true lifetime soul mate helped speed things up," she taunted back. Then she felt ashamed. Whatever had happened, Margaret was still the woman with whom she had shared five years of her life.

Cody took a step forward. "Let's call it a day. I'm still your friend, Margaret, and if you ever truly need a friend, look me up." Margaret's bottom lip was quivering and Cody touched her arm lightly. "And as a friend, I'm going to ask you to do something when you get back home."

"What?" Margaret asked dully.

"Go and get some counseling," Cody said. "I can get you the name of an excellent therapist. Janet told me about her."

Margaret looked sullen. "I'll think about it," she said. "Although I find the lesbian perspective very narrow and limiting."

Cody sighed. "Whereas the heterosexual perspective is so liberating and value-free."

Margaret shuffled awkwardly as Cody moved toward the front door.

"If you need to get back to Rarotonga for any reason, there's a flight every second afternoon," Cody said. "Just phone me." She indicated the old party line telephone in the hallway. "Turn the handle once."

"I understand," Margaret said in a low voice.

Cody escaped out the door and jumped lightly off

the verandah. Then she turned and looked up at the bemused expression on her former lover's face.

No, she didn't understand, Cody thought with a rush of sadness. She didn't understand at all.

Three days later Cody was on page 90 of her thriller, and Annabel still hadn't returned. The sky was as blue as ever but there was a curious heaviness in the air and the gulls seemed noisier than usual, wheeling expectantly above her and gathering in shrill cliques along the beach.

Amanda Valentine, Private Eye, was in a tight spot with some drug crazed psycho.

"Blowing you away won't exactly break my heart, dirtball," she yelled, crouched low behind the forklift.

She hoped Jesse Brown wasn't expecting company. She'd wasted a round already and at six bucks a throw that was one too many for scum like him.

"So watcha waitin' for, bitch?" the quarry bellowed.

Amanda caught a blur of denim behind a container to her left and followed it, bracing the Smith & Wesson against her rock-steady forearm.

Punks like Brown could sometimes be egged into mistakes. Bearing that in mind she tightened her finger around the trigger and taunted, "You better hope your brain's bigger than your dick, sonny."

Then she squeezed.

A shadow fell across the page. Startled, Cody looked up. It was Margaret again. Her heart sank.

"Hi," she greeted her, lukewarm.

Margaret mumbled a hello and flopped down onto the sand, removing her sunglasses. "I just wanted to let you know I'm leaving tomorrow," she said flatly. "I'll spend the rest of my vacation over on Rarotonga."

Cody nodded but did not speak.

Margaret squinted out to sea. "I thought about what you said," she began in a rush. "And I'd like the name of that therapist."

Cody sat up slowly, conscious of Margaret's extreme unease and the tell-tale puffiness around her eyes. For a moment guilt stabbed at her. Perhaps she'd been too hard on her.

"Sure," she said gently. "I'll drop Janet a line and ask her to call you."

"Thanks." Margaret trickled sand between her fingers. "Cody, I've been a fool," she said. "And I don't know how I can ever make it up to you. I still feel confused about my sexuality, but regardless of that I can see I behaved like a deadshit. I'm really sorry."

Cody took her hand and touched it to her cheek. "I was very hurt," she admitted. "But I do care about you, Margaret. Five years doesn't vanish overnight."

"Oh, Cody." There was hope in Margaret's eyes. "Could we ..."

Cody shook her head quickly. "It's too late Margaret. There's no going back. In some ways I feel like a different person now and I'll bet you do too."

"I feel older, I'm not so sure about wiser, though," Margaret joked weakly.

Cody felt a surge of relief at that hint of her ex-lover's old sense of humor. "We had some great times together, Margaret," she said.

"Yes." Margaret's voice wavered and she stooped forward, shoulders heaving. "I don't know what went wrong, Cody," she sobbed. "It was like one day I woke up and I just couldn't get any vision of the future, of us as old people. All I could think of was husband and wife, parents, children, grandparents, nuclear families — and I've been feeling frightened ever since. I don't want to be lonely when I'm old. I need people ... family."

"Of course you do." Cody put an arm around her shoulders. "It's not a crime to want that, Margaret. But role models of old lesbian couples and lesbian families are in short supply." She added grimly, "Anyone would think we spontaneously combust at age fifty or something."

"Yet there are masses of older women around," Margaret said. "Some of them must be lesbians."

"Of course they are," Cody agreed. "But old women are invisible at the best of times, especially in terms of their sexuality. Many are very closeted and I'm sure some are not even aware they *are* lesbian."

"At least it won't be that way for our generation," Margaret said.

Cody tried not to show her skepticism. "I hope you're right. We certainly do have a few more options about how we choose to live now. They may not be easy options, but they're what we've got, and I guess if we want anything to change, it's up to us, isn't it?"

She gave Margaret a quick hug. "Thanks for dropping by. I hope you enjoy Rarotonga."

Margaret gave her a watery smile and a kiss on the cheek. "Will you ring me when you get back?"

"Of course I will," Cody promised and as she watched Margaret trudge off down the beach, she released a long deep sigh.

Since their conversation when Margaret first arrived, Cody had rifled through her feelings again and again, seeking the slightest evidence that she might want to give the relationship another chance. She could find none, and if anything, her resolve was strengthened — even if she never saw Annabel again, Cody realized she would not go back to Margaret.

CHAPTER FOURTEEN

Annabel gazed up at the sky with ill-concealed frustration. "Looks okay to me, Bevan," she said.

The pilot shrugged impassively. "Sure does . . . at the moment."

"We've got hours before it hits and I have to get back to the island and batten down the hatches."

"I radioed this morning and Cody's got all of that under control."

"Cody . . ." Annabel bit back the urge to ask about her.

"Smart cookie, that one," he said. "The place has been running like a well-oiled machine."

Annabel frowned at him and tried not to feel irrational envy at the idea of anyone having seen Cody regularly for the past fortnight, especially a man.

She indicated the Dominie. "So how long before she's ready?"

Bevan waved his mechanic over. "Ms. Worth is pining to fly the silver sky, my friend. What news of the maimed bird?"

John Smith wiped his hands on the rag dangling from his back pocket and sucked in his breath wetly. "Bout another two hours guvnor, and that's without testing 'er."

"You hear the forecast?"

"Yep. Reckon it's the big one this time."

"Hurricane Mary," Bevan mused out loud. "She's five hundred miles northeast and nowhere to go but here."

"Gulls are in," Smithy said, indicating the noisy ranks congesting the tarmac.

Bevan lit a cigarette and turned to Annabel. "We won't be flying today," he said bluntly. As Annabel glared across his shoulder at the forlorn Dominie, he went on, "Even if we get the new struts welded we're not going to have enough time to test her before the storm hits."

"How long do we need, for God's sake?"

"We'd have to circle Raro a couple of times, put down and inspect her. That's at least another two hours on top of repair time. We'll never make it, kid."

Annabel glanced at her watch and scanned the sky again. The horizon was condensing into a deep bruised purple and the air felt thick and humid. Bevan was right. They would never get to Moon Island in time. The hurricane would get there hours before it reached Rarotonga. She wondered briefly whether Silk & Boyd had a freighter leaving, and contemplated heading into Avarua to check them out.

Bevan seemed to read her mind. "All shipping's canceled," he said dryly, "and air traffic's been diverted. You're lucky you got here when you did."

Annabel snorted. "I guess that's one way of looking at it," she muttered. "I'm sure a hurricane fetishist would be thrilled. Anyway," she noted with a frown, "isn't it unusual to have one at this time of year?"

"Sure is," Bevan agreed. "Round here most of the action happens November to March."

"That's mid-summer?"

Bevan nodded. "Mid-summer to autumn, the wet season."

"So how long before it gets here?"

"Depends how fast she's moving. The tide's way up. Another few hours and we'll get the outer winds here. She'll hit Moon Island way before then, of course."

Annabel chewed her lip and shoved her hands into her pockets in a gesture of frustration. If only she'd come back a little sooner — not that traveling from Boston to the Cook Islands was exactly a garden party. It had taken nearly three days, with four changes of plane and a sticky overnighter on Tahiti.

For a moment she felt a pang of homesickness. It had been so reassuring to slip into the comfortable routine of a Boston week, catch up with friends, wander the Freedom Trail like a tourist. Somehow the city had seemed more relaxed than she remembered, or perhaps it was just her. Boston was beautiful in the summer, the cobblestones mellow and warm, yachts bobbing on the Charles River.

To Annabel's surprise she had actually enjoyed herself spending whole days in her mother's company. She had survived shopping expeditions to Newberry Street and lunch at the Ritz Carlton with Laura and her cronies. She had listened to her mother complain about the Desecration of Our National Heritage in Back Bay without once defending her own apartment.

For the first time in her life, Annabel was aware of feeling totally relaxed around Laura, unafraid to be herself. She sensed it was different for her mother too. It was as though each of them was taking tiny tentative steps toward the other, creating safe passage across uncharted emotional territory.

As they drew closer, it pained Annabel deeply to look back at her childhood and realize how much she had missed out on, how badly she had been affected by an agenda she had known nothing about, a lie lived by the people who loved her best. The veiled comments and underground messages were not her imagination. She was not paranoid or hysterical. There was nothing wrong with her. There never had been.

Annie was gone. She grieved for her — for the relationship that might have been. Yet at the same time, she began to feel curiously light. It was such a relief to know the truth. That she was Annie's daughter. That Annie had loved her.

Now, as she came to terms with her grief, she suddenly saw a future she could never have imagined — a relationship with Laura on a whole new basis. How strange it was, she thought. In losing a mother, she had found one too.

When Laura had kissed her goodbye at the airport and said come home soon, Annabel knew she meant it and had said impulsively, "I'd like to bring a close friend."

Her mother had looked a little nervous. "A woman friend?"

"Yes. Her name is Cody ... er Cordelia."

Laura gave a quick nod. "I shall look forward to meeting her."

It was a little stiff but the genuine openness in her eyes had both startled and touched Annabel and she had hugged her warmly.

Recalling that hug, Annabel felt a rush of emotion for Laura — her mother. Love. It was the simplest truth of all.

She looked again at the congealing horizon and cursed the weather. Short of swimming, there was no way she could get to Moon Island now. Damn, Annabel thought angrily, trying not to entertain even for a second the idea that something might happen to Cody.

Bevan must have glimpsed her expression, for he delivered a comradely slap across the shoulders. "She'll manage," he said and something in his voice caught her attention.

He knew. Annabel was immediately uncomfortable. Then she glanced at the pilot and comprehension slowly dawned. Bevan was gay. The man he lived with on Atiu was his partner. Annabel felt like an idiot. Why hadn't she clicked sooner? Stereotypes, she thought cynically.

Bevan was a tough flier with a past she knew better than to inquire about. He was tall and lean, a kind of dog-eared version of Robert Redford. Yet what had she expected a gay man to look like? No one she knew conformed to the hairdresser stereotype.

For that matter, what was a lesbian supposed to look like? Annabel thought about her own appearance and almost laughed. Bloody stereotypes. "Let's go hole up at the Banana Court," she said cheerlessly.

"Sounds good to me." Bevan stubbed out his cigarette and paced around the Dominie. "Time to tuck her up, Smithy."

The wiry little mechanic shook his head. "I'll carry on if yer don't mind, guvnor. I'd like to see 'er airworthy before the storm 'its. You never know," he added obscurely.

Annabel pulled off her light jacket and tossed it over her bags. "Smithy's right," she said briskly. "Let's get her in shape. The Banana Court will still be there tonight."

They all looked at each other and Annabel grimaced. "Tempt fate, why don't you," she muttered wryly.

Bevan was fiddling with the radio set against the wall and Annabel felt her heart leap as she caught the sound of static, then Cody's voice drifting in and out of range. "Moonbase to shuttle Dominie. Moonbase calling Dominie, do you read me?"

"Roger, I read you Moonbase. Over," Bevan responded.

"When do you expect touchdown Dominie? The natives are getting restless. Over."

Annabel exchanged a look with Bevan and hurried over to take the handpiece. "Not today Moonbase," she said huskily. "We have a gravity problem. Over."

More static, then, "Annabel, you're back!"

"Just in time to be too late, it seems. Over."

"But when are you coming?" Cody sounded panicky and Annabel was aware of the handpiece sliding in her wet palm. She felt sick at heart, desperate to be on her island, to be with Cody. "We're not going to make it before the storm hits. Are you okay? Over."

There was a pause. The radio whistled and Annabel frantically twisted the dials. "I wish you were here," Cody's voice faded in and out.

"Me too," Annabel said hollowly. "I'll make it up to you. I promise. Over."

"Oh, Annabel," Cody said. "I've missed you so much. Over."

Annabel noticed Bevan had moved discreetly to the plane and was helping Smithy with a welding iron. "I have to go and help the others," she said firmly. "But I'll be over as soon as we can get off the ground. What are your plans for the storm? Over."

Cody immediately sounded more confident. "It's

already started raining here, and the wind is getting pretty bad." The transmission had become miraculously clear. "Mrs. Marsters went back to Rarotonga yesterday and I've evacuated all the guests to Villa Luna. We're going to spend the night in the Kopeka Cave. I walked Kahlo in with the supplies this morning and we're all loading up to leave now. Over."

Annabel heaved a sigh of relief. The cave was a perfect shelter. It was only a bit over an hour's walk from Villa Luna across the *makatea,* a fossilized coral reef now covered in jungle. Like many on the neighboring islands, the cave was a nesting place for hundreds of tiny Kopeka birds. Cody and Annabel had picnicked there one day and Annabel had been amazed at the chambers full of stalactites and curious limestone formations. One even had human bones in it and Mrs. Marsters had explained that it was an ancient burial chamber for the one-time inhabitants of Moon Island, and very *tapu,* or sacred.

"That's a great idea," Annabel said. "Be careful, won't you. The *makatea*'s sharp."

"We will," Cody promised and said something else that was lost in a flurry of static.

Annabel quickly adjusted the frequency. "Cody . . ." She felt awkward. "I know this is silly, but if anything goes wrong I just wanted you to know you mean a lot to me. Over."

"I'm crazy about you too, Annabel," Cody said back through the fading signal. "Please be careful. This is hard. Over."

"Have fun camping out. I'll see you tomorrow, hopefully. Bye darling. Over and out."

Both women sat for a long moment staring at their crackling radio sets and feeling stupid for wanting to cry.

Overhead the sky darkened and a few hundred miles away, above a warm oily sea, Hurricane Mary gathered strength.

"I remember Tracy," a loud Australian slurred. "Back in seventy-four. Christ mate, smashed Darwin to bits. Christmas bloody Day, too."

"Peace on earth, eh mate?" a man near him mumbled into his Fosters.

Annabel sipped her coconut water and peered gloomily toward the main road. It was the usual Friday night carnage: drunken drivers jockeying their Subarus around the Post Office roundabout, Honda two-strokes polluting the air faster than you could breathe it and the occasional Banana Court patron lying down on the road in a stupor.

The *Cook Island News* informed Annabel that a panty thief at large in Avarua was found to be Mr. Jimmy Tuara's goat, and that the New Zealand Prime Minister had resigned and his successor was a man with a big appetite but no children.

The local radio was ordering everyone under cover and inland. Meteorologists were evidently predicting the hurricane would bypass Rarotonga and that the island would only experience its fringe winds. But Bevan was not convinced.

"I've got the jeep outside," he told Annabel. "I think it's time we got to the hotel."

Annabel nodded absently. "I wonder how Cody is

getting on," she said, imagining her huddled in a sleeping bag in the Kopeka Cave.

Thank God they'd made radio contact. Ironically, that was one debt they owed to the freak weather conditions, according to Bevan. Normally Moon Island was out of range.

Bevan was climbing up onto a chair. "Rarotongan Resort Hotel," he shouted into the din. "Anyone need a lift?"

A woman materialized at their table as they were preparing to leave.

"Have you got room for me?" she asked nervously and Annabel caught her breath as she recognized the accent. The woman was a New Zealander, and very attractive, with curly red hair and dark blue eyes.

"Sure," Annabel said.

The woman followed them outside. "By the way, I'm Margaret," she said as they climbed into the back of the jeep.

Annabel introduced herself and Bevan, and made an obvious remark about the weather.

The woman looked up at the sky and shuddered. "We get a lot of wind back home. But never a hurricane."

"You're a New Zealander?" Annabel asked conversationally.

"Yes. I'm from Wellington. That's the capital city."

Wellington. Annabel's eyes darted to the woman. "What do you think of Rarotonga?" she inquired cautiously.

"It's beautiful," Margaret enthused. "Although I liked Moon Island better."

"You've been on Moon Island?"

"Yes. For a week." She sounded wistful and Annabel tried to ignore the sudden alarm that clutched her stomach.

"There's another New Zealander on the island . . ." she began.

Margaret's eyes widened. "Do you know Cody?" she asked. "Cody Stanton?"

"Yes," Annabel said flatly. This woman knew Cody. Her name was Margaret and she had just spent a week on the island. Annabel tried not to draw conclusions but it seemed obvious that their passenger was Cody's ex-lover.

It had started to rain but the air still felt unbearably thick, and Annabel couldn't help but notice the way Margaret's T-shirt clung to her full breasts and that her hair was curling into wonderful little ringlets. She was quite stunning, Annabel thought, feeling colorless by comparison.

"How did you get to meet Cody?" Margaret was asking.

"I live on Moon Island," Annabel explained. "As a matter of fact, Cody has been filling in for me recently, while I was back home in Boston."

Her voice fell slightly short of normal and Margaret looked at her intently. Then she said, "Are you lovers?"

Annabel nearly spluttered and her glance flew to Bevan then returned, shocked, to Margaret. Margaret nodded knowingly. "You are," she observed. "That was quick work."

Annabel moistened her lips and for the first time that day she was grateful for the dark sky. Why the hell did she feel guilty? she thought angrily. Cody and Margaret had broken up before Cody had arrived on the island and Margaret was certainly not a woman wronged.

"I guess Cody will have told you about us, then," Margaret said.

Annabel squirmed in her seat. "She mentioned her relationship had broken up," she said evasively and wished she could end the conversation.

"I was a fool," Margaret said. "I came over to get her back."

"I see." Annabel felt like she was walking on nails. "Look, Margaret, I really don't feel comfortable discussing this. It's between you and Cody —" She broke off as they drew up alongside the hotel.

Rain was now falling in dense sheets and a strong wind bent the palm trees. A sign at reception warned guests to stay indoors until further notice and the lobby was filled with excited tourists acting as if a tropical hurricane was yet another thrilling attraction on their holiday of a lifetime.

Although she could see Margaret wanted to continue their conversation, Annabel immediately excused herself and escaped to her room, a jumble of thoughts chasing each other in her head.

Long-term relationships went through bad patches, everyone knew that. Couples could often heal their differences and carry on. Perhaps this was the very process Cody and Margaret were going through. Perhaps she should take a step back right now and give Cody some room. And save herself getting hurt in the bargain.

Annabel peeled off her damp clothes and headed

into the compact bathroom to stand under the shower. Cody had said she was crazy about her. That was all very well in the heat of the moment. Short flings could often be very passionate. Women could become infatuated. And after all, in an environment like Moon Island, it was easy to forget there was a world beyond the horizon. It was easy to exist only for the present. I've been through that pattern, Annabel reminded herself. It was classic rebound drama.

As she dried herself she pictured Cody, remembering the last time they'd made love, and her skin tingled. Whatever was happening for Cody, Annabel suddenly recognized with dazzling clarity was what was happening for her. She was falling in love. Cody was not just convenient instant gratification. Annabel had experienced the McDonald's approach to lesbian relationships — eat and run, as she'd once put it to a friend. She wanted something different this time, yet she was oddly scared by the idea. And Cody. What did she want?

ta. ta. ta. ta. ta.

Cody twisted in her sleeping bag and changed position, stretching her cramped limbs. The four women in the cave were sitting in a close huddle around Cody's attempt at a fire and Kahlo was tethered in the adjoining chamber.

Outside the sky was black and the noise of the

hurricane was deafening. It filtered through with the distortion of an outdoor rock concert. Cody was astounded at the range of sounds, everything from a deep low bass to screams that made *Nightmare on Elm Street* sound like a Mormon Tabernacle Choir rehearsal. Dust was falling in clouds from the cave roof, and its resident Kopekas clicked and swooped like thousands of tiny bats.

"Yuk!" A small blonde woman batted ineffectually at them. "These birds give me the creeps. How long is this going to last, anyway?" Dawn, a young Australian, had complained non-stop ever since they had left Villa Luna.

"That depends on the size of the hurricane," Cody responded patiently. "According to the radio the winds will be at their worst for six hours. After that . . ." She shrugged. "I guess we'll just have to hope there's something left of the houses."

"You're exaggerating!" Dawn accused.

Brenda, an older woman, rolled sympathetic eyes at Cody. "Since when have you become an expert on hurricanes, Dawn?" she remarked with gentle irony.

Dawn prodded the fire and said nothing.

Cody wriggled out of her sleeping bag. "I'm going to take a look."

"I'll join you." Another of their party scrambled up. "I could do with stretching my legs."

"Are you sure that knee of yours is okay?" Cody eyed the woman uncertainly. Catherine had fallen as they crossed the *makatea* and the razor sharp coral had sliced her leg open in a jagged line from her knee to her calf. Her jeans were stiff with drying blood and Cody was worried the wound would open again if she moved.

"I think so." Catherine tested her leg gingerly. "You did a pretty good job of sticking it together."

Cody took her arm and they made their way slowly toward the mouth of the cave.

"The truth is," Catherine admitted as soon as they got out of earshot, "I couldn't stand another moment of listening to that spoiled brat whining on. If she says another word about demanding a refund when she gets home I'm going to stuff her Reeboks down her throat."

Cody laughed. "She's just a kid, Catherine. And she's really scared. I think she complains all the time because it gives her something to think about, gets her mind off her fear."

"You're far too nice," Catherine muttered. "If it wasn't for you, the silly little bitch would have been mincemeat crossing the ridge. And she's not the least bit grateful."

"Ignorance is bliss," Cody said. "Anyway, I think I'd rather have her grumbling and in one piece than chopped up and screaming."

"You ought to make *her* piggyback *you* going back," Catherine said darkly.

Cody shook her head. "I plan to get there."

"Do you think there'll be anything left ... really?"

"I honestly don't know." Cody squinted out at the chaos beyond the cave. "It's pretty bad out there. I reckon those winds must be over a hundred miles an hour."

Catherine shuddered. "Thank God we came here."
With some difficulty she lit a cigarette.

"Your cottage won't survive," Cody said. "It's too
close to the beach." She thought regretfully of pretty
little Frangipani Cottage, the one person villa in
Hibiscus Bay. The beaches on the northeastern side
of the island would be the worst hit.

Catherine had been staying over there for the
past week and Cody had enjoyed visiting her to drop
off supplies. To her amazement she had discovered
that Catherine, a fellow Wellingtonian, lived only a
few streets away from Cody's old flat in Hataitai.
Yet they'd had to travel thousands of miles to meet.

"So what difference will being on the beach
make?" Catherine was asking. "The wind's the same
everywhere, isn't it?"

"More or less," Cody said. "But it's the storm
surge that's the biggest worry. That's a kind of tidal
wave that comes in just as the hurricane strikes.
They were talking about it on the radio. That's why
I decided to move us all inland."

"Do you mean half the island might be under
water even when we get out of here?" Catherine
sounded shocked.

"It's possible," Cody conceded. "But I'll go out by
myself for a scout around before we all head back."

Catherine puffed agitatedly on her cigarette.
"Does this all mean what I think? That we could be
stranded here for days with no supplies and no idea
when anyone will get to us?"

"Let's hope not," Cody said as cheerfully as she
could. "But if we are, then we'll just have to make
the best of it." God, she sounded like a Girl Guide
leader.

Catherine groaned loudly. "Well, Dawn will really have something to complain about then."

     🐦 🐦 🐦 🐦 🐦

"That is a horrible sound," Annabel said, pushing her meal half-heartedly around her plate. It was her favorite — *maroro,* or flying fish. One of the few authentic Polynesian dishes on a menu clearly designed for carnivorous Westerners.

Brandi's was packed, and looking around, Annabel couldn't help but be reminded of the carnival atmosphere of a *Poseidon Adventure.* She shivered at the idea.

"Collective madness," Bevan remarked, verbalizing her sentiments. "They're tossing down cocktails like there's no tomorrow."

"Damned fools," Annabel muttered. Like most New Englanders, she had a healthy respect for storms. Her mother had been a child in the 1938 hurricane and had returned from vacationing on Westhampton Beach only days before the great gale hit. The family's house had been completely destroyed, earning Laura the childhood nickname "Lucky" for getting out in time.

Family legend had it that the shock had been so great for Annabel's grandmother that it had set her health into a decline. She had died, leaving fourteen-year-old Laura to manage the household.

Recently Annabel had wondered how much this experience had contributed to her mother's over-developed sense of responsibility and her obvious insecurity about close relationships. Annabel was conscious of an echo of this pattern in her own reluctance to commit herself. Something her mother said came back to her — *Everyone I love leaves.*

On some level, Annabel realized, that was exactly what she expected too. She thought about a little girl called Lucy whose two mothers had left her — one in body, the other in mind. So now she was the one who did the leaving — with her behavior over the past four years since Clare, and in preparing to do the very same thing with Cody, using Margaret as an excuse.

"Idiot," she murmured.

Bevan nodded agreement. "Let's hope none of them is called on to make like a hero," he commented, eyeing a particularly raucous bunch of tourists.

Annabel followed his gaze and grimaced. Four drunk men were showing off to the women at their table.

"Reckon we should leave the sheilas here and go take a squiz down the beach, mate," one large member of the group slurred loudly. There was general agreement and they got to their feet and lurched off.

"Bloody lemmings," Bevan hissed and pulled his chair out.

"You're not going after them!" Annabel protested, then swallowed her irritation. If Bevan chose to take responsibility for some of the more limited members of his sex, that was his funeral. On the other hand, she needed an experienced pilot. "Just don't go outside, will you?" she ordered.

Bevan stubbed out his cigarette with an

impassive expression. "You're the boss," he said mildly and left her.

An hour later, when he hadn't returned, Annabel was trying not to panic. Brandi's had subsided into a moribund hush, the diners no longer able to compete with the awesome roar outside the hotel walls. The band strummed "Staying Alive" with all the enthusiasm of an undertaker's convention and Annabel stared into her drink and fought off images of Moon Island decimated, Cody maimed, or dead. She should have taken her to Boston, told her what was going on. Suddenly the entire soap opera seemed mere trivia and what mattered most of all was life ... and love.

Rebecca had left Moon Island thirty years ago without Annie, and they had never seen each other again. Annabel couldn't bear to contemplate history repeating itself, and she felt tears plop onto her hands.

"Cheer up."

It was a woman's voice and Annabel looked up sharply to see a stranger sitting opposite her. She was very tanned, with short, greying black hair and a hard-looking body clad in white shirt and black pants. Very nice too, Annabel thought abstractly.

"I see your fellow's got himself lost," she observed.

Annabel stiffened. "You noticed," she said coolly.

The woman grinned. "You looked like you could use some company and I thought I'd beat the hunk over there."

Annabel followed her gesture and met the

bloodshot eyes and encouraging nod of a balding man in a Hawaiian shirt.

"Oh great," she muttered and quickly looked away.

"My name's Rose," said the stranger in a near-Texas drawl. "Rose Beecham."

"I'm Annabel Worth."

"I've seen you fly that Dominie," the woman remarked, moving a little closer to make herself heard above the din of the storm.

"You have?" Annabel was surprised.

"When I first got here," Rose explained. "Originally I'd planned to stay on Moon Island but you were booked out. I thought I'd check again when I arrived and they said I could find you flying the island shuttle. So I went for a look and ran into some old dude who couldn't speak a word of English." She spoke completely deadpan and Annabel burst out laughing.

"That was Smithy," she said. "And he's as English as they come. London, no less.

"No doubt the confusion was mutual. He was acting like I was off another planet." Rose Beecham laughed from low in her belly and her dark blue eyes ran over Annabel appreciatively. "So who's the cowboy you were with?"

Annabel gave her a measuring look, then told herself not to be so prickly. So what if a dyke tried to pick her up in the middle of a tropical hurricane? It wasn't as if she had anything else planned. "That was Bevan Mitchell. He owns the Dominie and flies for me."

"And you own Moon Island, right?"

Annabel nodded, a little bemused at the third degree.

"Can I buy you a drink?" Rose offered, summoning the waiter.

"Pineapple juice," Annabel said and Rose ordered the same.

"Is your hair natural?" she asked Annabel bluntly, then said, "Sorry. Betcha get real sick of that kind of question."

Annabel relaxed. "Mostly people don't ask. They stare instead."

"Well, I can sure understand that," Rose said. "You're mighty pleasing to the eye."

Annabel blushed, sipped her pineapple juice and tried to frame a gentle but definite brush-off. Then she froze as an unearthly boom erased every other sound and the restaurant shuddered as though in an earthquake.

Then everything went black and people were screaming. Annabel felt her arms grabbed, and Rose's voice in her ear ordered, "Don't panic. Come with me."

Rose had her firmly about the waist and was also gripping one hand with powerful fingers. "Let's move our asses out of here."

"Where are we?" Annabel shouted as they reached a door.

"My room's right out there."

"No!" Annabel shook herself free and staggered back a step.

The building shuddered again and Annabel clutched Rose automatically.

"If we go now, we can do it," Rose urged.

"Otherwise we can head back to that watering hole and get ourselves trampled to death. Take your pick."

Three hours later, while the hurricane pillaged the island with random cruelty, Annabel lay in Rose's arms and marveled at the twist of fate that saw her telling a total stranger her most guarded secrets.

"It would make a great book," Rose said when Annabel had finished telling her about Aunt Annie. "Wrong genre for me, of course."

Annabel stirred. "You're a writer?"

"Sure am, honey."

"I'm impressed," said Annabel. "Is that why you're over here? To research a book?"

"Hell, no. I came for some peace and quiet. And the one-night stand of a lifetime."

Annabel spluttered. "You're joking!"

"Nope," said Rose. "When I saw you flying that Dominie I said that's the one, and tonight in the restaurant I knew the goddess had delivered."

"Rose!" Annabel pulled back from the warm circle of her arms. "We're about to be blown off the island and you're propositioning me?"

"Yes I am," said Rose. "The way I see it, truth is stranger than fiction, honey. When you get asked what did you do in the hurricane and you say, I got picked up by some woman and we went up to her room for a quickie, what do you think they'll say?"

Annabel couldn't help but laugh.

"Who'd believe you?" Rose continued in her deep

easy drawl. *"Last Tango in Rarotonga — what a title."*

She rolled to face Annabel squarely. "This is a once-only opportunity. We can lie here all night wondering what it would be like and worrying about whether we'll see tomorrow, or we can have some truly excellent sex. Your choice, honey."

CHAPTER FIFTEEN

When Cody poked her head out of the cave at first light, she could only sense an incredible stillness. The air smelled green and woody. In the distance the sea pulsed softly. A breeze wandered across the *makatea,* but nothing moved. She blinked, stepped into the thin light.

The jungle had been laid to waste, trees uprooted, palms and undergrowth flattened. It looked as though some giant had kicked a drunken path across the land. Lonely clumps of trees stood dazed in the midst of the carnage, like soldiers in a spent battlefield, and birds perched silent and observant on torn branches.

Cody turned back into the cave. "You can go outside," she told the other woman. "But only in pairs and no more than a hundred yards from the cave. I'm going to Villa Luna to check the damage. If I'm not back by tomorrow morning, start making your own way. I'll leave a trail in the difficult patches. Just remember, once you get over the ridge, head straight for the sea."

"I don't think we should move until you get back here," Dawn broke in. "Catherine can hardly walk and I can't possibly cross that coral by myself."

"You won't be by yourself, Dawn," Brenda reminded her crisply. "You'll have us."

"Oh terrific!" a petulant Dawn responded. "A cripple and a granny."

"Dawn!" Cody pulled her up short. "Here." She thrust a water canteen at the pouting blonde. "You're in charge of this. Keep it filled. You'll find plenty of rainwater trapped everywhere."

"Well if that's the case then I don't see why I need to fill the damn thing up all the time," she whined.

Cody suppressed a strong urge to slap some sense into her. She didn't want to have to explain her worst fears, that she might find the houses razed and radio contact lost, that there was every chance they could be stranded without water or supplies for days, weeks even, until help arrived. It would all depend on what had happened on Rarotonga and Cody could hardly bear to think about that.

Keeping her temper in check, she passed her compass to Catherine. "Take this as well. Villa Luna is approximately an hour and a half west of here. If you have to go it alone, walk slowly and take turns carrying the supplies."

Cody had just finished cleaning and dressing Catherine's leg wound and she knew it needed medical attention. The first aid kit contained only a tiny tube of antiseptic cream and Cody had used most of it already. Besides, they needed something stronger. Wounds infected overnight in this heat and Catherine's looked angry already. It must be painful, Cody thought. She wished she could offer some relief.

"I'll be all right," Catherine said, as though she'd read her mind, and Cody threw her a grateful look.

She left them standing forlornly in front of the cave, Dawn sulking, Brenda philosophical, and Catherine looking decidedly stressed.

Checking her bearings with the sun, she took Kahlo's reins and led the mare carefully out across the *makatea* toward the ridge that separated them from the sea. She was almost too scared to climb it. God only knew what she might find on the other side.

࿔ ࿔ ࿔ ࿔ ࿔

Annabel and Rose kissed chastely, as though last night had never happened. The walkway outside Rose's room was a sea of bags, bedding and dazed hotel patrons. Windows had smashed in several rooms and hotel staff were attempting to remove some of the debris.

"I'm going to take a walk," Annabel said. "I've got to find Bevan."

"And I think I'd better line up for the phone," said Rose.

Rose smiled her slow easy smile, eyes sparkling Kodachrome blue, and she took Annabel's hand briefly. "Your Cody's one lucky lady," she said and Annabel flushed.

"And you oughtn't to waste yourself on one-nighters, Rose," she told the older woman.

"Was last night a waste?" Rose inquired softly.

Annabel felt her knees weaken a little. "Last night was great," she confessed. "I'll never forget it."

They kissed again and crossed the courtyard in companionable silence. Rose left Annabel fighting for elbow room in the mob at reception and wondering how on earth the harassed staff could be expected to cope with hordes of tourists asking impossible questions. When was the next flight to Sydney? Was my pearl earring found in the restaurant last night? If I post this letter today when will it be delivered?

Annabel was beginning to question the usefulness of leaving a message for Bevan when, from somewhere behind, a woman called her name breathlessly and Margaret squeezed her way to her side.

"Is Cody all right?" she asked urgently. "Have you heard from her?"

Annabel bit back her annoyance, reminding herself that this woman had spent five years with Cody. It was entirely reasonable for her to be concerned for her safety. "No I haven't. But I'm sure she'll be fine and as soon as I can I'll be flying out to the island."

Margaret nodded, then looked a little flustered. "I'm sorry about yesterday," she said. "Ever since I got here all I seem to have done is open my mouth to change feet."

Annabel shrugged it off. "No problem." She wished Margaret would just go away.

"You might like to know that I'm going home the minute I can get a plane out of here," Margaret informed her. "I just wanted to wish you luck."

"Luck?" Annabel echoed.

"With Cody," she explained. "It's all over between us, in case you hadn't worked that out."

Annabel lifted questioning eyes and Margaret met them with a hint of pain in her own. "That's what I was trying to tell you," she said. "I came here to get her back and she turned me down."

"Because of me?" Annabel asked carefully.

Margaret shook her head. "I don't think so. Cody's not into games. She doesn't love me any more and she said so."

Annabel scrutinized Margaret's face. Why was Cody's ex bothering to tell her this?

As though to answer her, Margaret touched her arm very lightly and said, "Last night I wondered if I was going to be killed, or maybe Cody was, and I guess it made me think about a few things, helped me get my priorities straight."

Annabel nodded. "I think I know what you mean."

"Then I guess I've said enough." Margaret removed her hand a little self-consciously and smiled at Annabel. "Give Cody my love," she said. "And be happy, won't you." She stepped back and was quickly lost in the anxious crowd choking the lobby.

Annabel turned her attention back to the task at hand with a sinking heart. While she and Margaret had been talking they had gradually been pushed further away from the front desk as people stepped in front of them. Now she would be waiting for hours.

To hell with Bevan Mitchell, she thought crossly. She would go down to the hanger right now and fly the Dominie herself. As she spun round, her shoulder was tapped.

"You!" she gasped as the object of her wrath grinned sheepishly. Relief flooded her and she clutched his arm. "Thank God you're all right. I was so worried."

"I'm overwhelmed," Bevan commented.

Recovering herself quickly, Annabel gave a snort. "You're lucky you're not fired," she tossed back and glared pointedly at him. "You've got a black eye!"

"You should see them," Bevan said.

Annabel shook her head, appalled. "You didn't fight with those, those ... cretins?"

"Not exactly," Bevan responded. "I told them they had two choices. Stay inside, or stay inside tied up. Being Australian, the silly bastards couldn't figure out which was the more intelligent. I had to stay there until it was safe, in case they needed untying in a hurry."

Annabel rolled her eyes expressively. "Men!" she said with disgust. "We're getting wiped out by a hurricane and the boys are playing Rambo. Come on." She started toward the door. "Let's get out to the airport."

Bevan lit a cigarette and looked at his watch. "Smithy should be there by now." Annabel noticed a grimness in his voice. "I don't think we'll be flying, though."

"Is it still too windy?"

Bevan shook his head as they got aboard the jeep. "Look around, Annabel," he said. "If it's anything like this we'll be lucky to have a plane."

"Someone up there was lookin' out for us guvnor," Smithy noted as the three of them inspected the Dominie. The hangar, apart from the loss of half its roof, was in remarkably good shape and the plane itself was untouched.

Annabel ran her fingers across the smooth silver fabric of a wing in wonderment. The area surrounding the terminal, and Avarua itself, was a shambles. Her heart had sunk when she took in the full extent of the devastation.

"The poor islanders," she said. "At least all the tourists can go home and brag about their big adventure at the next office lunch, but what about the locals?"

"They'll get aid," Bevan said. "But it won't be enough of course. Hundreds of families have lost everything, including their clothes."

"There's three dead in Avarua," Smithy commented.

"Names?" Bevan peered out from under the plane.

"Not yet," Smithy told him.

"Your place?" Bevan queried. Smithy had a little villa southwest of Avarua.

"Just lost the roof. Day's work, that's all guv."

"What about the other islands — any reports?" Annabel asked him.

"They reckon six dead on Atiu."

Bevan's head jerked up and Smithy spread his hands. "No names yet. Bloody tidal wave flattened the place. Heard nothing from Moon either."

"Can we fly this afternoon?"

Smithy shook his head. "Runway's like a bomb-site and all air traffic's grounded till further notice."

"But what about rescue flights?" Annabel insisted.

"New Zealand's sending in a few Army choppers and Silk and Boyd are heading out for the Northern Group this afternoon."

"But we have to get to the island," Annabel insisted, hands on hips. "After all, we've got *tourists* to rescue."

They all knew what she was saying. The islanders could wait, but foreign tourists were the Cook Island's livelihood.

"I shall convey that laudable sentiment to our Police Chief, Annabel," Bevan said very seriously. "God forbid that we have *rich* foreign ladies roughing it *alone* on those inhospitable shores."

"Shocking," Smithy shook his head. "Could end up with *casualties* ..."

"Big insurance companies investigating for negligence ..." Bevan added.

"Sleazy," Annabel commented. "Very sleazy. When do we see him?"

* * * * *

Annabel pulled on her bomber jacket and settled into her seat next to Bevan.

"No heroics if we dump her," the pilot said very seriously. "This runway's a disaster and God only knows what the strip will be like at the other end. Are you sure you want to come?"

Annabel threw him a sharp look. At least Bevan could relax, knowing Don was all right on Atiu. But so far, no one had been able to make contact with Moon Island.

Smithy pulled away the chocks and they taxied towards the runway.

"This thing would go up in sixty seconds," Bevan went on tersely. "She's all skin. So if we take a spill, bail out and run as fast as you can. Don't wait for me. Got it?"

"Got it," Annabel said coolly. "Same goes for you."

"Sure." Bevan built the revs and Annabel closed her eyes and held her breath.

They made it into the air on their first attempt, and then Annabel could see how it was that Bevan had managed a successful operation in a war zone. He had treated the pot-holes and debris on the runway with scorn, and it was only when they'd safely climbed to two thousand feet that he casually broke the bad news.

"I think we've damaged the undercarriage. Can you take a look?"

She matched his cool. "Sure." She clambered around in the rear of the cabin, peering out the windows. "One of the wheels is all bent. What are we going to do?"

He shrugged. "Land and fix it."

"Land?" Annabel shivered. "But how can we?"

"Well, we certainly can't stay up here all day," he pointed out dryly.

Annabel took their bearings and calculated an estimated time of arrival. "ETA thirteen hundred hours," she told Bevan.

The pilot responded with a grin.

"That gives you a whole hour to get your affairs in order."

"Bastard," said Annabel.

When they came in sight of Moon Island Annabel almost cried with relief. It was still there, exactly where the map said. Idiot, she told herself. Bevan made a low pass over Passion Bay and Annabel peered down at the carnage of broken palm trees and debris piled on the beach. They climbed and circled over the island.

From five hundred feet overhead Annabel told Bevan she was certain she'd seen a movement on the *makatea* not far from Villa Luna.

"Definite signs of life," Annabel said with relief. "They'll get to Villa Luna by the time we land."

"If we land," Bevan muttered.

They banked steeply over the strip, both peering down.

"It's not too bad. Looks almost like someone's cleared it." There was relief and puzzlement in his voice.

Annabel was also baffled. The strip looked like a freshly swept patch of floor in the midst of an expanse of litter. "Weird," she remarked. "Do you think the women have done it?"

Bevan shrugged. "Maybe. Or else Mr. Big is

looking after us. It's sure as hell going to make the difference between flying and frying with this damned wheel shot. Let's take her in."

They climbed quickly and turned into the wind to prepare for landing. Annabel tightened her belt and braced herself as they dropped out of the sky. Bevan seemed to be making the descent at a peculiar tilt, the nose too far up.

Annabel started to panic.

"Bevan!" she cried. "Straighten up!"

He elbowed her roughly away, shouting, "Get down in the plane and get ready to jump."

Annabel obeyed blindly, screaming as they crashed down hard on the tail. The little plane bounced once, then veered into a spin, tried to straighten and bounced again frantically from side to side, wingtips just brushing the earth.

As the spinning slowed and Bevan killed the engines, Annabel smelled petrol, released the hatch and clambered back to Bevan.

"Go!" he shouted, but she had already released his belt and grabbed his arm to heave him roughly after her. They jumped in quick succession, rolled, and sprinted for the cover of the torn jungle, diving then belly-crawling as fast as they could.

After a couple of minutes lying with their heads covered, Bevan hissed. "You shouldn't have done that. I told you to get out."

"Crap!" Annabel lifted her head indignantly. "Anyway, I want you to teach me how to land on one wheel like that."

"The lady's gone troppo, old son," Bevan said tapping his head to illustrate the point. Then he got to his knees to peer across at the Dominie.

Annabel followed suit and grinned widely. Definite petrol fumes, but no flames.

"Time for a cigarette, eh Mitchell?" she joked, and received a filthy look.

"Planning to die young are we?"

After another five minutes they got up and cautiously approached the battered biplane. It had run off the strip and was leaning drunkenly against a palm stump, a large fabric tear on one wing fluttering in the Moon Island breeze like a surrender flag.

"You poor old thing," Annabel said and flicked a propeller affectionately.

"I think she'll live," Bevan declared as he knelt down beside the undercarriage. "Whether I can fix this is another matter," he went on, but Annabel was no longer listening.

She was watching a figure emerge from the jungle at the opposite end of the strip. It appeared to be carrying something large.

"Cody!" Annabel yelled and she was running before she even became conscious of the fact. The figure lowered her load to the ground and stretched out her arms.

"Annabel." Cody caught her, stumbled back a step and overbalanced and the two women fell laughing and crying to the ground.

They lay there crushed together and gazing into each other's eyes as though they could never see enough.

"I love you," Annabel said.

"I love you too," Cody told her.

After a long moment just holding each other, they managed to stumble to their feet. Holding hands, they started across the strip. Then Cody remembered.

"My barrel." She hurried back and hoisted the cumbersome wooden keg into her arms. The top was fractured and several of the struts were loose.

"What on earth ..." Annabel began.

"I found it when I was cleaning up the strip. And since the water pump isn't working, I got kind of worried in case you ..."

"Crashed?"

Cody glanced towards the Dominie. "That landing ..."

Annabel smiled. "Creative, wasn't it?"

Cody and Annabel left Bevan to sort out the Dominie and headed for Villa Luna. The house had lost its verandah and part of its roof, but otherwise it appeared to be remarkably intact. They reached the front door just in time to hear a loud petulant complaint from within.

"All I can get is a pile of static. The fucking thing must be broken."

Annabel looked startled and Cody raised a quietening hand. "Dawn," she whispered. Obviously the young woman was none the worse for wear.

"They must have landed by now," another voice said. Brenda.

"Well, one of us is going to have to find that bloody strip and I guess it'll have to be me."

Could anyone sound resentful and pleased all at once, Cody wondered. Dawn certainly gave it her best shot.

"Look after her," she ordered Brenda and Cody felt a stab of alarm. Catherine's leg.

Dawn was talking. "That bloody Cody Stanton.

She's definitely been here. That bed's been slept in and her T-shirt's on the floor in there. She's probably sunbathing on the beach or something while we're half dead. Just wait till I find her. She's really asking for it ..."

Annabel raised expressive eyebrows and Cody grimaced. "Looks like I'm dogfood," she mouthed.

"A bloody knuckle sandwich," the litany continued then footsteps sounded. Cody and Annabel jumped guiltily to one side.

A very cross-looking young woman emerged and dropped from the doorway to the ground. To Cody's amusement Dawn didn't even see her and Annabel, but started straight off toward the jungle in the opposite direction from the strip.

She was filthy, jeans and T-shirt torn and covered in sweat and jungle stains. Her wavy honey-colored hair was matted and tied back into a sorry ponytail with a shoelace that looked like one of Catherine's fluorescent orange specials.

Cody took a couple of paces forward and said softly, "Dawn, you're going the wrong way."

The woman stopped in her tracks and spun round. "You!" she burst out. "Where the fuck have you been?" Her face was a picture. Anger, relief and mortification all at once. Then she hurtled and threw her arms around a startled Cody.

"You're all right," she wailed. "We were so worried, and Catherine's leg is all swollen, and we got lost. It was awful." She wiped her running eyes and nose on her fist then slapped Cody with both hands, sobbing. "Where were you? You promised you'd come back."

Cody grabbed her hands and led the overwrought

young woman over to Annabel. "Dawn, I'm here now, and you made it all on your own. That was really brave."

She sat Dawn down under the remains of a frangipani tree and gave her shoulders an encouraging squeeze. "Sit out here with Annabel and relax. I'm going inside to look at Catherine's leg."

"We've got a full medical kit in the plane," Annabel put in as Cody walked toward the house.

They were both surprised when Dawn scrambled back up, dusted herself off and said. "I'll get it. Which way do I go?"

Annabel opened her mouth to give directions, thought again and said, "Follow me."

It was nearly daybreak when Annabel and Cody finally crawled exhausted into bed.

Dawn, Brenda and Catherine were bunked down in the guest room and Bevan in the lounge. They had patched the roof as best they could with wood and leaves.

Fortunately the Dominie's medical kit was well equipped with local anesthetic, antibiotics and surgical instruments, and Bevan and Cody between them had stitched Catherine's leg where the wound had reopened. Bevan, Cody had discovered, was often called on by the islanders if a doctor wasn't available. He was a trained paramedic and had told Cody that since flying the island, he had also acquired a specialty in emergency pig surgery.

After Catherine had been made comfortable with pain-killers, Cody, Annabel and Bevan had met to devise a plan for getting everyone off the island and back to Rarotonga.

"What a day!" Cody snuggled against Annabel and sighed contentedly. "I wish I had some energy left," she murmured.

Annabel stroked her face lovingly. "Me too ... but we'd better get some sleep. We've got a heap of work to do tomorrow ... today."

"I can't believe all this has happened," Cody said. "Twenty-four hours just doesn't seem long enough for a hurricane, a plane crash and major surgery."

Annabel smiled at the embellishments then said, "A month doesn't seem long enough to have had my whole life turned upside down. I haven't even had a chance to tell you about it all."

"Me neither," said Cody. "I hardly know where to begin."

"We've got plenty of time," Annabel said and kissed her gently. "I want us to be together always. We belong together."

Cody felt a rush of emotion at Annabel's words. She'd experienced that same sense. Of belonging with Annabel. Of destiny throwing them together from continents apart. At times it seemed so bizarre and unlikely, that it was almost beyond belief. Cody had been made redundant the day Annabel's aunt had died. If Cody's employer hadn't made a mistake with zeros she would never have dreamed of "escaping" to an island, if Margaret hadn't left her ... if ...

"We were meant to be together," she murmured sleepily. "I tried to run away, but I couldn't."

"Me too." Annabel nodded, rocked her slowly, kissed her eyelids closed. "I love you," she whispered.

And while they slept in each other's arms, an innocent breeze stirred the palms on Passion Bay and the island awoke to an untroubled horizon.

EPILOGUE

A year later in a Back Bay apartment, Annabel Worth slid onto her lover's knee and bit her neck softly. "What's the book, sweetheart?"

"It's the latest Amanda Valentine," Cody enthused. "And guess what. It's set in Rarotonga! Hey!" she objected as Annabel whipped the book out of her hands and scanned the opening lines.

The second Amanda Valentine laid eyes on Lucy Jones she knew she was looking at trouble. But she liked what she saw anyway.

Lucy was sitting two tables down, mutilating a fish.

With mounting disbelief, Annabel snapped the book shut and examined the jacket as though it were alive with crawling things. *Last Tango in Rarotonga* by Rose Beecham, and an artist's impression of the Rarotongan Resort Hotel on a stormy night.

"So what do you think of it?" she asked Cody faintly.

"It's great," Cody pronounced. "Although a bit far-fetched, especially that first scene when she meets Lucy and they jump straight into bed. Right in the middle of a hurricane. I mean, *really!*"

Cody rolled her eyes and Annabel dropped the book back into her lover's lap, snuggling closer and smiling at a private joke.

"You know, Cody Stanton," she said, sliding her hands under Cody's T-shirt. "I love you."

PAINTED MOON by Karin Kallmaker. 224 pp. Delicious Kallmaker romance. ISBN 1-56280-075-2 — $9.9.

THE MYSTERIOUS NAIAD edited by Katherine V. Forrest & Barbara Grier. 320 pp. Love stories by Naiad Press authors. ISBN 1-56280-074-4 — 14.9:

BODY GUARD by Claire McNab. 208 pp. A Carol Ashton Mystery. 6th in a series. ISBN 1-56280-073-6 — 9.9:

CACTUS LOVE by Lee Lynch. 192 pp. Stories by the beloved storyteller. ISBN 1-56280-071-X — 9.9:

SECOND GUESS by Rose Beecham. 216 pp. An Amanda Valentine Mystery. 2nd in a series. ISBN 1-56280-069-8 — 9.9:

THE SURE THING by Melissa Hartman. 208 pp. L.A. earthquake romance. ISBN 1-56280-078-7 — 9.9:

A RAGE OF MAIDENS by Lauren Wright Douglas. 240 pp. A Caitlin Reece Mystery. 6th in a series. ISBN 1-56280-068-X — 9.95

TRIPLE EXPOSURE by Jackie Calhoun. 224 pp. Romantic drama involving many characters. ISBN 1-56280-067-1 — 9.95

UP, UP AND AWAY by Catherine Ennis. 192 pp. Delightful romance. ISBN 1-56280-065-5 — 9.95

PERSONAL ADS by Robbi Sommers. 176 pp. Sizzling short stories. ISBN 1-56280-059-0 — 9.95

FLASHPOINT by Katherine V. Forrest. 256 pp. Lesbian blockbuster! ISBN 1-56280-043-4 — 22.95

CROSSWORDS by Penny Sumner. 256 pp. 2nd Victoria Cross Mystery. ISBN 1-56280-064-7 — 9.95

SWEET CHERRY WINE by Carol Schmidt. 224 pp. A novel of suspense. ISBN 1-56280-063-9 — 9.95

CERTAIN SMILES by Dorothy Tell. 160 pp. Erotic short stories. ISBN 1-56280-066-3 — 9.95

EDITED OUT by Lisa Haddock. 224 pp. 1st Carmen Ramirez Mystery. ISBN 1-56280-077-9 — 9.95

WEDNESDAY NIGHTS by Camarin Grae. 288 pp. Sexy
adventure.   ISBN 1-56280-060-4   10.95

SMOKEY O by Celia Cohen. 176 pp. Relationships on the playing
field.   ISBN 1-56280-057-4   9.95

KATHLEEN O'DONALD by Penny Hayes. 256 pp. Rose and
Kathleen find each other and employment in 1909 NYC.
                                        ISBN 1-56280-070-1   9.95

STAYING HOME by Elisabeth Nonas. 256 pp. Molly and Alix
want a baby . . . or do they?   ISBN 1-56280-076-0   10.95

TRUE LOVE by Jennifer Fulton. 240 pp. Six lesbians searching for
love in all the "right" places.   ISBN 1-56280-035-3   9.95

GARDENIAS WHERE THERE ARE NONE by Molleen Zanger.
176 pp. Why is Melanie inextricably drawn to the old house?
                                        ISBN 1-56280-056-6   9.95

MICHAELA by Sarah Aldridge. 256 pp. A "Sarah Aldridge"
romance.   ISBN 1-56280-055-8   10.95

KEEPING SECRETS by Penny Mickelbury. 208 pp. A Gianna
Maglione Mystery. First in a series.   ISBN 1-56280-052-3   9.95

THE ROMANTIC NAIAD edited by Katherine V. Forrest &
Barbara Grier. 336 pp. Love stories by Naiad Press authors.
                                        ISBN 1-56280-054-X   14.95

UNDER MY SKIN by Jaye Maiman. 336 pp. A Robin Miller
mystery. 3rd in a series.   ISBN 1-56280-049-3.   10.95

STAY TOONED by Rhonda Dicksion. 144 pp. Cartoons — 1st
collection since *Lesbian Survival Manual.*   ISBN 1-56280-045-0   9.95

CAR POOL by Karin Kallmaker. 272pp. Lesbians on wheels
and then some!   ISBN 1-56280-048-5   9.95

NOT TELLING MOTHER: STORIES FROM A LIFE by Diane
Salvatore. 176 pp. Her 3rd novel.   ISBN 1-56280-044-2   9.95

GOBLIN MARKET by Lauren Wright Douglas. 240pp. A Caitlin
Reece Mystery. 5th in a series.   ISBN 1-56280-047-7   9.95

LONG GOODBYES by Nikki Baker. 256 pp. A Virginia Kelly
mystery. 3rd in a series.   ISBN 1-56280-042-6   9.95

FRIENDS AND LOVERS by Jackie Calhoun. 224 pp. Mid-western
Lesbian lives and loves.   ISBN 1-56280-041-8   9.95

THE CAT CAME BACK by Hilary Mullins. 208 pp. Highly praised
Lesbian novel.   ISBN 1-56280-040-X   9.95

BEHIND CLOSED DOORS by Robbi Sommers. 192 pp. Hot, erotic
short stories.   ISBN 1-56280-039-6   9.95

CLAIRE OF THE MOON by Nicole Conn. 192 pp. See the movie —
read the book!   ISBN 1-56280-038-8   10.95

SILENT HEART by Claire McNab. 192 pp. Exotic Lesbian
romance.   ISBN 1-56280-036-1   10.95

HAPPY ENDINGS by Kate Brandt. 272 pp. Intimate conversations
with Lesbian authors.   ISBN 1-56280-050-7   10.95

THE SPY IN QUESTION by Amanda Kyle Williams. 256 pp. 4th
Madison McGuire.   ISBN 1-56280-037-X   9.95

SAVING GRACE by Jennifer Fulton. 240 pp. Adventure and
romantic entanglement.   ISBN 1-56280-051-5   9.95

THE YEAR SEVEN by Molleen Zanger. 208 pp. Women surviving
in a new world.   ISBN 1-56280-034-5   9.95

CURIOUS WINE by Katherine V. Forrest. 176 pp. Tenth
Anniversary Edition. The most popular contemporary Lesbian
love story.   ISBN 1-56280-053-1   10.95

CHAUTAUQUA by Catherine Ennis. 192 pp. Exciting, romantic
adventure.   ISBN 1-56280-032-9   9.95

A PROPER BURIAL by Pat Welch. 192 pp. A Helen Black
mystery. 3rd in a series.   ISBN 1-56280-033-7   9.95

SILVERLAKE HEAT: A Novel of Suspense by Carol Schmidt.
240 pp. Rhonda is as hot as Laney's dreams. ISBN 1-56280-031-0   9.95

LOVE, ZENA BETH by Diane Salvatore. 224 pp. The most talked
about lesbian novel of the nineties!   ISBN 1-56280-030-2   9.95

A DOORYARD FULL OF FLOWERS by Isabel Miller. 160 pp.
Stories incl. 2 sequels to *Patience and Sarah.*   ISBN 1-56280-029-9   9.95

MURDER BY TRADITION by Katherine V. Forrest. 288 pp. A
Kate Delafield Mystery. 4th in a series.   ISBN 1-56280-002-7   9.95

THE EROTIC NAIAD edited by Katherine V. Forrest & Barbara Grier.
224 pp. Love stories by Naiad Press authors.   ISBN 1-56280-026-4   13.95

DEAD CERTAIN by Claire McNab. 224 pp. A Carol Ashton
mystery. 5th in a series.   ISBN 1-56280-027-2   9.95

CRAZY FOR LOVING by Jaye Maiman. 320 pp. A Robin Miller
mystery. 2nd in a series.   ISBN 1-56280-025-6   9.95

STONEHURST by Barbara Johnson. 176 pp. Passionate regency
romance.   ISBN 1-56280-024-8   9.95

INTRODUCING AMANDA VALENTINE by Rose Beecham.
256 pp. An Amanda Valentine Mystery. First in a series.
                                            ISBN 1-56280-021-3   9.95

UNCERTAIN COMPANIONS by Robbi Sommers. 204 pp.
Steamy, erotic novel.   ISBN 1-56280-017-5   9.95

A TIGER'S HEART by Lauren W. Douglas. 240 pp. A Caitlin
Reece mystery. 4th in a series.   ISBN 1-56280-018-3   9.95

PAPERBACK ROMANCE by Karin Kallmaker. 256 pp. A
delicious romance.   ISBN 1-56280-019-1   9.95

MORTON RIVER VALLEY by Lee Lynch. 304 pp. Lee Lynch at
her best! ISBN 1-56280-016-7   9.95

THE LAVENDER HOUSE MURDER by Nikki Baker. 224 pp. A
Virginia Kelly Mystery. 2nd in a series. ISBN 1-56280-012-4   9.95

PASSION BAY by Jennifer Fulton. 224 pp. Passionate romance,
virgin beaches, tropical skies. ISBN 1-56280-028-0   9.95

STICKS AND STONES by Jackie Calhoun. 208 pp. Contemporary
lesbian lives and loves. ISBN 1-56280-020-5   9.95

DELIA IRONFOOT by Jeane Harris. 192 pp. Adventure for Delia
and Beth in the Utah mountains. ISBN 1-56280-014-0   9.95

UNDER THE SOUTHERN CROSS by Claire McNab. 192 pp.
Romantic nights Down Under. ISBN 1-56280-011-6   9.95

RIVERFINGER WOMEN by Elana Nachman/Dykewomon.
208 pp. Classic Lesbian/feminist novel. ISBN 1-56280-013-2   8.95

GRASSY FLATS by Penny Hayes. 256 pp. Lesbian romance in
the '30s. ISBN 1-56280-010-8   9.95

A SINGULAR SPY by Amanda K. Williams. 192 pp. 3rd Madison
McGuire. ISBN 1-56280-008-6   8.95

THE END OF APRIL by Penny Sumner. 240 pp. A Victoria Cross
Mystery. First in a series. ISBN 1-56280-007-8   8.95

A FLIGHT OF ANGELS by Sarah Aldridge. 240 pp. Romance set at
the National Gallery of Art ISBN 1-56280-001-9   9.95

HOUSTON TOWN by Deborah Powell. 208 pp. A Hollis Carpenter
mystery. Second in a series. ISBN 1-56280-006-X   8.95

KISS AND TELL by Robbi Sommers. 192 pp. Scorching stories by
the author of *Pleasures*. ISBN 1-56280-005-1   9.95

STILL WATERS by Pat Welch. 208 pp. A Helen Black mystery.
2nd in a series. ISBN 0-941483-97-5   9.95

TO LOVE AGAIN by Evelyn Kennedy. 208 pp. Wildly
romantic love story. ISBN 0-941483-85-1   9.95

IN THE GAME by Nikki Baker. 192 pp. A Virginia Kelly
mystery. First in a series. ISBN 1-56280-004-3   9.95

AVALON by Mary Jane Jones. 256 pp. A Lesbian Arthurian
romance. ISBN 0-941483-96-7   9.95

STRANDED by Camarin Grae. 320 pp. Entertaining, riveting
adventure. ISBN 0-941483-99-1   9.95

THE DAUGHTERS OF ARTEMIS by Lauren Wright Douglas.
240 pp. A Caitlin Reece mystery. 3rd in a series.
ISBN 0-941483-95-9   9.95

CLEARWATER by Catherine Ennis. 176 pp. Romantic secrets
of a small Louisiana town. ISBN 0-941483-65-7   8.95

THE HALLELUJAH MURDERS by Dorothy Tell. 176 pp. A Poppy
Dillworth mystery. 2nd in a series. ISBN 0-941483-88-6   8.95

SECOND CHANCE by Jackie Calhoun. 256 pp. Contemporary
Lesbian lives and loves. ISBN 0-941483-93-2   9.95

BENEDICTION by Diane Salvatore. 272 pp. Striking,
contemporary romantic novel. ISBN 0-941483-90-8   9.95

BLACK IRIS by Jeane Harris. 192 pp. Caroline's hidden past . . .
ISBN 0-941483-68-1   8.95

TOUCHWOOD by Karin Kallmaker. 240 pp. Loving, May/
December romance. ISBN 0-941483-76-2   9.95

COP OUT by Claire McNab. 208 pp. A Carol Ashton mystery.
4th in a series. ISBN 0-941483-84-3   9.95

THE BEVERLY MALIBU by Katherine V. Forrest. 288 pp. A
Kate Delafield Mystery. 3rd in a series. ISBN 0-941483-48-7   10.95

THAT OLD STUDEBAKER by Lee Lynch. 272 pp. Andy's affair
with Regina and her attachment to her beloved car.
ISBN 0-941483-82-7   9.95

PASSION'S LEGACY by Lori Paige. 224 pp. Sarah is swept into
the arms of Augusta Pym in this delightful historical romance.
ISBN 0-941483-81-9   8.95

THE PROVIDENCE FILE by Amanda Kyle Williams. 256 pp.
Second Madison McGuire ISBN 0-941483-92-4   8.95

I LEFT MY HEART by Jaye Maiman. 320 pp. A Robin Miller
Mystery. First in a series. ISBN 0-941483-72-X   9.95

THE PRICE OF SALT by Patricia Highsmith (writing as Claire
Morgan). 288 pp. Classic lesbian novel, first issued in 1952 . . .
acknowledged by its author under her own, very famous, name.
ISBN 1-56280-003-5   9.95

SIDE BY SIDE by Isabel Miller. 256 pp. From beloved author of
Patience and Sarah. ISBN 0-941483-77-0   9.95

STAYING POWER: LONG TERM LESBIAN COUPLES
by Susan E. Johnson. 352 pp. Joys of coupledom.
ISBN 0-941-483-75-4   12.95

SLICK by Camarin Grae. 304 pp. Exotic, erotic adventure.
ISBN 0-941483-74-6   9.95

NINTH LIFE by Lauren Wright Douglas. 256 pp. A Caitlin
Reece mystery. 2nd in a series. ISBN 0-941483-50-9   8.95

PLAYERS by Robbi Sommers. 192 pp. Sizzling, erotic novel.
ISBN 0-941483-73-8   9.95

MURDER AT RED ROOK RANCH by Dorothy Tell. 224 pp.
A Poppy Dillworth mystery. 1st in a series. ISBN 0-941483-80-0   8.95

LESBIAN SURVIVAL MANUAL by Rhonda Dicksion.
112 pp. Cartoons! ISBN 0-941483-71-1   8.95

A ROOM FULL OF WOMEN by Elisabeth Nonas. 256 pp.
Contemporary Lesbian lives. ISBN 0-941483-69-X 9.95

THEME FOR DIVERSE INSTRUMENTS by Jane Rule. 208
pp. Powerful romantic lesbian stories. ISBN 0-941483-63-0 8.95

LESBIAN QUERIES by Hertz & Ertman. 112 pp. The questions
you were too embarrassed to ask. ISBN 0-941483-67-3 8.95

CLUB 12 by Amanda Kyle Williams. 288 pp. Espionage thriller
featuring a lesbian agent! ISBN 0-941483-64-9 8.95

DEATH DOWN UNDER by Claire McNab. 240 pp. A Carol
Ashton mystery. 3rd in a series. ISBN 0-941483-39-8 9.95

MONTANA FEATHERS by Penny Hayes. 256 pp. Vivian and
Elizabeth find love in frontier Montana. ISBN 0-941483-61-4 8.95

LIFESTYLES by Jackie Calhoun. 224 pp. Contemporary Lesbian
lives and loves. ISBN 0-941483-57-6 9.95

WILDERNESS TREK by Dorothy Tell. 192 pp. Six women on
vacation learning "new" skills. ISBN 0-941483-60-6 8.95

MURDER BY THE BOOK by Pat Welch. 256 pp. A Helen
Black Mystery. First in a series. ISBN 0-941483-59-2 9.95

THERE'S SOMETHING I'VE BEEN MEANING TO TELL
YOU Ed. by Loralee MacPike. 288 pp. Gay men and lesbians
coming out to their children. ISBN 0-941483-44-4 9.95

LIFTING BELLY by Gertrude Stein. Ed. by Rebecca Mark. 104
pp. Erotic poetry. ISBN 0-941483-51-7 8.95

AFTER THE FIRE by Jane Rule. 256 pp. Warm, human novel
by this incomparable author. ISBN 0-941483-45-2 8.95

THREE WOMEN by March Hastings. 232 pp. Golden oldie. A
triangle among wealthy sophisticates. ISBN 0-941483-43-6 8.95

PLEASURES by Robbi Sommers. 204 pp. Unprecedented
eroticism. ISBN 0-941483-49-5 8.95

EDGEWISE by Camarin Grae. 372 pp. Spellbinding
adventure. ISBN 0-941483-19-3 9.95

FATAL REUNION by Claire McNab. 224 pp. A Carol Ashton
mystery. 2nd in a series. ISBN 0-941483-40-1 8.95

KEEP TO ME STRANGER by Sarah Aldridge. 372 pp. Romance
set in a department store dynasty. ISBN 0-941483-38-X 9.95

IN EVERY PORT by Karin Kallmaker. 228 pp. Jessica's sexy,
adventuresome travels. ISBN 0-941483-37-7 9.95

OF LOVE AND GLORY by Evelyn Kennedy. 192 pp. Exciting
WWII romance. ISBN 0-941483-32-0 8.95

CLICKING STONES by Nancy Tyler Glenn. 288 pp. Love
transcending time. ISBN 0-941483-31-2 9.95

SURVIVING SISTERS by Gail Pass. 252 pp. Powerful love
story.   ISBN 0-941483-16-9   8.95

SOUTH OF THE LINE by Catherine Ennis. 216 pp. Civil War
adventure.   ISBN 0-941483-29-0   8.95

WOMAN PLUS WOMAN by Dolores Klaich. 300 pp. Supurb
Lesbian overview.   ISBN 0-941483-28-2   9.95

THE FINER GRAIN by Denise Ohio. 216 pp. Brilliant young
college lesbian novel.   ISBN 0-941483-11-8   8.95

OCTOBER OBSESSION by Meredith More. Josie's rich, secret
Lesbian life.   ISBN 0-941483-18-5   8.95

BEFORE STONEWALL: THE MAKING OF A GAY AND
LESBIAN COMMUNITY by Andrea Weiss & Greta Schiller.
96 pp., 25 illus.   ISBN 0-941483-20-7   7.95

OSTEN'S BAY by Zenobia N. Vole. 204 pp. Sizzling adventure
romance set on Bonaire.   ISBN 0-941483-15-0   8.95

LESSONS IN MURDER by Claire McNab. 216 pp. A Carol
Ashton mystery. First in a series.   ISBN 0-941483-14-2   9.95

YELLOWTHROAT by Penny Hayes. 240 pp. Margarita, bandit,
kidnaps Julia.   ISBN 0-941483-10-X   8.95

SAPPHISTRY: THE BOOK OF LESBIAN SEXUALITY by
Pat Califia. 3d edition, revised. 208 pp.   ISBN 0-941483-24-X   10.95

CHERISHED LOVE by Evelyn Kennedy. 192 pp. Erotic
Lesbian love story.   ISBN 0-941483-08-8   9.95

THE SECRET IN THE BIRD by Camarin Grae. 312 pp. Striking,
psychological suspense novel.   ISBN 0-941483-05-3   8.95

TO THE LIGHTNING by Catherine Ennis. 208 pp. Romantic
Lesbian 'Robinson Crusoe' adventure.   ISBN 0-941483-06-1   8.95

DREAMS AND SWORDS by Katherine V. Forrest. 192 pp.
Romantic, erotic, imaginative stories.   ISBN 0-941483-03-7   8.95

MEMORY BOARD by Jane Rule. 336 pp. Memorable novel
about an aging Lesbian couple.   ISBN 0-941483-02-9   9.95

THE ALWAYS ANONYMOUS BEAST by Lauren Wright
Douglas. 224 pp. A Caitlin Reece mystery. First in a series.
                                          ISBN 0-941483-04-5   8.95

PARENTS MATTER by Ann Muller. 240 pp. Parents'
relationships with Lesbian daughters and gay sons.
                                          ISBN 0-930044-91-6   9.95

MAGDALENA by Sarah Aldridge. 352 pp. Epic Lesbian novel
set on three continents.   ISBN 0-930044-99-1   8.95

THE BLACK AND WHITE OF IT by Ann Allen Shockley.
144 pp. Short stories.   ISBN 0-930044-96-7   7.95

SAY JESUS AND COME TO ME by Ann Allen Shockley. 288
pp. Contemporary romance.   ISBN 0-930044-98-3   8.95

LOVING HER by Ann Allen Shockley. 192 pp. Romantic love
story.   ISBN 0-930044-97-5   7.95

MURDER AT THE NIGHTWOOD BAR by Katherine V.
Forrest. 240 pp. A Kate Delafield mystery. Second in a series.
                                          ISBN 0-930044-92-4   10.95

WINGED DANCER by Camarin Grae. 228 pp. Erotic Lesbian
adventure story.   ISBN 0-930044-88-6   8.95

PAZ by Camarin Grae. 336 pp. Romantic Lesbian adventurer
with the power to change the world.   ISBN 0-930044-89-4   8.95

SOUL SNATCHER by Camarin Grae. 224 pp. A puzzle, an
adventure, a mystery — Lesbian romance.   ISBN 0-930044-90-8   8.95

THE LOVE OF GOOD WOMEN by Isabel Miller. 224 pp.
Long-awaited new novel by the author of the beloved *Patience
and Sarah*.   ISBN 0-930044-81-9   8.95

THE HOUSE AT PELHAM FALLS by Brenda Weathers. 240
pp. Suspenseful Lesbian ghost story.   ISBN 0-930044-79-7   7.95

HOME IN YOUR HANDS by Lee Lynch. 240 pp. More stories
from the author of *Old Dyke Tales*.   ISBN 0-930044-80-0   7.95

PEMBROKE PARK by Michelle Martin. 256 pp. Derring-do
and daring romance in Regency England.   ISBN 0-930044-77-0   7.95

THE LONG TRAIL by Penny Hayes. 248 pp. Vivid adventures
of two women in love in the old west.   ISBN 0-930044-76-2   8.95

AN EMERGENCE OF GREEN by Katherine V. Forrest. 288
pp. Powerful novel of sexual discovery.   ISBN 0-930044-69-X   9.95

THE LESBIAN PERIODICALS INDEX edited by Claire
Potter. 432 pp. Author & subject index.   ISBN 0-930044-74-6   12.95

DESERT OF THE HEART by Jane Rule. 224 pp. A classic;
basis for the movie *Desert Hearts*.   ISBN 0-930044-73-8   10.95

TORCHLIGHT TO VALHALLA by Gale Wilhelm. 128 pp.
Classic novel by a great Lesbian writer. ISBN 0-930044-68-1   7.95

LESBIAN NUNS: BREAKING SILENCE edited by Rosemary
Curb and Nancy Manahan. 432 pp. Unprecedented autobiographies
of religious life.   ISBN 0-930044-62-2   9.95

THE SWASHBUCKLER by Lee Lynch. 288 pp. Colorful novel
set in Greenwich Village in the sixties. ISBN 0-930044-66-5   8.95

TOTTIE by Sarah Aldridge. 181 pp. Lesbian romance in the
turmoil of the sixties.   ISBN 0-930044-01-0   6.95

THE LATECOMER by Sarah Aldridge. 107 pp. A delicate love
story.   ISBN 0-930044-00-2   6.95

ODD GIRL OUT by Ann Bannon.   ISBN 0-930044-83-5   5.95
I AM A WOMAN 84-3; WOMEN IN THE SHADOWS 85-1;   each
JOURNEY TO A WOMAN 86-X; BEEBO BRINKER 87-8. Golden
oldies about life in Greenwich Village.

JOURNEY TO FULFILLMENT, A WORLD WITHOUT MEN, and   3.95
RETURN TO LESBOS. All by Valerie Taylor   each

These are just a few of the many Naiad Press titles — we are the oldest and
largest lesbian/feminist publishing company in the world. Please request a
complete catalog. We offer personal service; we encourage and welcome
direct mail orders from individuals who have limited access to bookstores
carrying our publications.